Born and educated in England, Nicolas Freeling now lives in France and writes like nobody else; much imitated but always ahead of the fashion; admired by all but there are always new surprises. 'Unique' is the word most generally used to describe his work. In a career of over thirty years he has gathered every honour and defied every convention of crime fiction.

D1464835

One More River

NICOLAS FREELING

WARNER BOOKS

A *Warner* Book

First published in Great Britain in 1998
by Little, Brown and Company

This edition published by Warner Books in 1999

Copyright © Nicolas Freeling 1998

The moral right of the author has been asserted.

All rights reserved.
No part of this publication may be reproduced,
stored in a retrieval system, or transmitted, in any
form or by any means, without the prior
permission in writing of the publisher, nor be
otherwise circulated in any form of binding or
cover other than that in which it is published and
without a similar condition including this
condition being imposed on the subsequent purchaser.

*All characters in this publication are fictitious
and any resemblance to real persons, living or dead,
is purely coincidental.*

A CIP catalogue record for this book is
available from the British Library.

ISBN 0 7515 2012 8

Typeset in Baskerville by M Rules
Printed and bound in Great Britain by
Mackays of Chatham plc

Warner Books
A Division of
Little, Brown and Company (UK)
Brettenham House
Lancaster Place
London WC2E 7EN

This book is dedicated to Tyrannosaurus Rex, the empire-builder who found there was nothing left to eat, and dropped dead in consequence.

> *'The animals went in two by two,*
> *Vive la Compagnie . . .*
> *. . . One More River –*
> *There's one more river to cross.'*

The empire's marching song was perfectly familiar to (and much parodied by) all schoolboys of John's generation and background.

PROLOGUE

This book, which is what it is, came as the saying goes '*into my hands*'. The italics denote an initial unease, because in fiction, and John was primarily a fiction writer, the phrase introduces a ploy or device, much employed in the nineteenth century; that of the tale told through letters or diaries, arranged with interpolations by a suppositious friend or relation who purports to 'edit' this material for public consumption.

John would not have allowed that. He would have been ribald. A good craftsman, he would have found other, simpler means of presenting this material. To my own mind it is a clumsy method. But I have no choice.

My name is Jonathan Wade; I am a literary agent. For twenty years I have handled the work of John Charles; he was one of 'my' writers, and a writer speaks of 'his' agent. The possessives are shorthand for a less simplistic relation which often includes friendship, trust, a certain intimacy. I appear in these pages, briefly, in an episode John would probably not have kept in a finished script. The detail shows that I am none too happy about accepting this task, which is mine by friendship. Many of these pages made painful reading.

They were 'the shape of a book'. At the start John took a new notebook; he used German desk-diaries of quite an elaborate nature, because they have a format suitable for slipping in to the 'sacoche'. I use this, John's own word, since 'handbag' has to the English ear an effeminate, even a Lady Bracknell sound, misleading to all who did not know him. It held a clutter of papers and several pens, for John was never without 'the notebook'; he was a compulsive writer. (Another of my authors, of a similar cast, finding himself in jail, wrote the first ten thousand words of a book on lavatory paper. John would have approved.)

It arrived by the ordinary post. A literary agency gets 'books' by every mail, in every shape and form, some wildly dotty in their search for novelty and their effort to catch the eye. Apart from the German postmark my secretary saw at once that this was out of the ordinary run.

The notebook is full of other writers, of reminders and citations, often of quotes direct from memory. John lived, as writers do, inside his own books, for they were his reality rather than the day to day humdrum of our own. His acceptance of reality came late. Too late, for others as well as himself.

I have spent many weeks with it. John's small squiggly handwriting was familiar to me, and his characteristic ellipses appeared also in his prolific letters, and even in his conversation. Eyestrain apart, this shorthand was not much more difficult than that of his admired and frequently cited Mr Pepys. To turn this into printable shape has been an often puzzling and exasperating but largely a mechanical chore, and also a labour of love. John was a writer of acknowledged distinction, with an individual prose style. After my long experience of his work, I feel that this is probably a fair version of his voice. Indeed much of this is a literal transcription of his 300 closely written manuscript pages. The often rambling thought, the dislocated syntax, the occasional bad grammar are his own. As are the frequent words of French or German: in the heat of the moment these came to him quicker than English now and then. Some of these have been kept; more would have been unnecessarily irritating.

Lastly, as will be seen, he varies from one paragraph to another between a first- and a third-person narration. He would have of course corrected this while writing a book. I have kept largely to his original, since I think it throws light upon the nature of his personality. He was a deeply divided man. Many have said 'a rift right down the middle'. This habit throws the undeniable fact into sharper relief. He was himself fond of the Kipling quotation about 'two sides to his head'. Certainly, he got them badly confused. It should be remembered that he was an old man and under much strain.

There are naturally other problems. One is to get clearance from his children. 'Jaimie' I do not know, and he seems to have little interest in his father's work. I must talk with Alan and with Cathy; they are not just mentioned in the script but given textual lines of dialogue. Likewise 'Brigitte' must be consulted, while such people as 'Kollo' might be sensitive to questions of libel! Sibylle, whom I knew and respected, is now free. Or I should have closed the notebook after the first few pages, and sent it to her with the briefest word of explanation as to how it came into my possession.

The major difficulty is the boy Christian himself. The last fifty pages of the notebook are in his attractively readable hand, square and black, unmistakably German. I should like to meet him. I do not feel sure that he would wish it. I think that legally speaking his sending me the notebook constitutes permission to print. A meeting could be arranged, with a little detective work such as he – and John – had done. I feel pretty sure that he intended a tribute to both his grandparents: to John also, after some thought, as well as to the beloved Sibylle.

I think I can do no better than reproduce his covering letter. This was in English.

Dear Mr Wade

I am sending you this book, enclosed, because I have found out that Mr Charles, my grandfather, would want you to see it. You might not know what happened because it didn't get into the press much.

My Aunt Sibylle was very dear to me. I think it is a real and big tragedy that they did not understand each other better. I am very unhappy at the part I played in this disaster. I do not make excuses for myself. You will say that we Germans always do. I ask you please to believe that this is not so. When I found out the truth it was too late.

I think we do not stop blaming ourselves for the past. This leads us often to kill ourselves. but this I don't believe has been anyone's Fault.

Yours faithfully.

This seems to me to call for a brief comment. First, that I have reproduced this because it belongs with the rest. At the end of the book will be found his own comment. 'I am the future.'

Second, I do not subscribe to the boastful xenophobia still so widespread, for which everything German is spoken of as 'Teutonic' or 'Prussian'. That mentality is as damaging as it is deplorable.

My belief, shared by others, is that we should bring this book on to the market. The technical difficulties are not great; a few liberties will be taken with names and places, to protect identities of people still living.

London 1997

PART ONE

'A Green Flash'

It was what the weather people called 'a regular autumn anticyclone'. Regular, yes; rare for it to be this strong and this long. Day after day of this still and sunny blessing. And this all across Europe. Elsewhere in the world there are daily earthquakes; hurricanes; volcanoes. One begins to ask what can we possibly have done to merit this, saying each day that it won't last, and it does. Good, it's the equinox any moment now, and that will mean storms.

Mists, yes. Gossamer; spiders showing great activity, which he found an improvement on wasps, slugs, and stinging flies, all thriving under modern conditions, which is more than one can say of people. Plenty of mellow fruitfulness, with a slight but nasty taint of diesel exhausts. Throughout Europe they've been getting the harvest in; a large one and of good quality. Was a time, they'd have gone to church to give thanks, because a good harvest meant a secure winter and seed for the spring. Now you hear only the computer, counting cash.

He had come home too, with some harvest. Stock it in the barn, and then go out in the garden, to enjoy. Refresh the tired soul, what! With

> *'The bucking beam-sea roll*
> *Of a black Bilbao tramp'*?

Very nice, Mr Kipling, but he preferred the garden. Graham had got it down to a small and rather nasty flat in Antibes. One hadn't Graham's tastes, nor for that matter his talents. One had acquired instead, many years ago, this smallish but pleasant country house, and from time to time one lived here. All alone. The occasional mistress; that much one shares with Graham. None right this minute.

Fairly delectable, though. There are in France two places officially called 'Belle-Ile'; en-mer, the island off southern Brittany, and en-terre in northern Brittany where the land is good. But there are plenty of places called by the local people 'Bella Isla' jokingly, but the reason is the same. This was one; upland, and all around there are sheltering mountains. Eroded, and the good soil has collected here in the valley. Too high for vines really, but on the southfacing slope the locals all have a patch. Ordinary years it makes a goodish, distinctive, drinkable white wine which you drink, but you wouldn't write home to Mother about it. In years like this one they hold the grapes on the vine till late, getting small and wrinkly but storing sugar. A 'Spätlese', a 'vin sur paille' which is outstanding: which is little known and there's not much of it. In the right frame of mind, Mr Peartree will offer him a glass. Made by his father; oh yes it will keep.

Just the other day, relishing a cutting phrase, a journalist in Lausanne spoke of the 'obsolete little kingdom'. He was talking about nuclear-power-France. Not about here. When the père-Poirier speaks of the house he says 'the new house'. Which was built in 1827. His own house, known as 'the little farm' is fifteenth-century, has its original walnut panelling, and he keeps a sharp eye out for termites.

So here he was. Sprawled upon the terrace. In a long chair. Yes, Monseigneur. Why not? This much anyhow was his, safe, certain. He had made himself a cup of tea. Extraordinary; you'd think it still summer: bumble bees and butterflies. Pull the chair out and stare into a clear deep madonna-blue sky. Well, hasn't one earned it? Moments of peace are the greatest possible rarity.

Stimulated he sat up because the tea was getting cold. There was a plant, a perfectly common-looking scrubby plant but foliage of pretty cut, nice white flowers, bee thinks so too. There was also a tree, one of the maples that he loves the best, a leaf of wonderful design and now one can see that it is October, for the nerves are still green while the palm has become bronze and the sharp-pointed tips are an orange flame. It will take a moment as always for the eye to overcome its laziness, flex its muscles; see. He sees a Cézanne, pure colour in subtle juxtapositions: mm, brushstrokes by God who is an even better painter. His eye travelled along the garden and up the long swelling slope to the woodland beyond. A view in itself nothing wonderful, but by him-and-none-other Cézanned, artfully landscaped with twenty and more maple varieties, perspectived singly or in groups to make the most of the painterly recession. One good job, anyhow, over these last thirty years. He had planted them all, himself, young subjects bought from the specialist in Somerset, and now that he's too old for any serious gardening one comes here specially for these October days. And in spring of course for the azaleas.

Something to be proud of? There was not much in his life he could feel proud of. Certainly he had never written a book to look at, later, with satisfaction.

Sibylle had never felt happy with his gardening mania – a very English passion. Had hated it, even.

"When you are standing there, it's as though you shut me out. I feel your will there, daring me to come out and remind you of my existence." Even now he has to make an effort, tighten his will into a deliberate refusal to see her there among the green massifs, a bit sweaty and hair untidy, flushed from bending, in one of her sudden furious attacks upon weeds. He picked up the tea things and walked resolutely into the house to wash them up and tidy them away.

When he came back the sun was setting; it was time for the green flash. There is a legend – some say it is true – that if one stands upon the cliffs at Etretat in Normandy while the sun is setting in the Channel, at the moment that the red disc sinks into the waves there will come a blink of green to fill the sky; the famous Rayon Vert. He does not know whether he believes in this or not: strangely enough, for he knows most of the corners of France, he has never been there. He supposes it might be so. The sky often is green after a sunset. The light on that coast is remarkable and has fascinated generations of painters. But a flash, a blink? One would have to question a meteorologist with local knowledge. It could hardly be aurora, could it? Said to be strongest in June.

Here, some hundreds of miles south, it is altogether different. An intense green that comes just before the twilight. And it isn't a blink; it can last up to nigh a quarter of an hour, a great emerald glow. The azalea flowers, which have the same colouring as the maples in autumn, become magically unearthly. The green, a viridian Cézanne could not encompass since his palette was inevitably chemical, spreads right up to the state's woodland crowning the brow of the hill, where it makes the recession into horizon-blue. And one will wait, suspended in magic, for the first cry of the owl. Still evening here has not a sober livery.

So that he had placed himself in the heart of the green, upon the fountain terrace. The water here pours over a large flat stone roughly the shape of an opened fan and drops in a thin pretty curtain to the pool below. But this – alas – is a mechanical device impelled by a hidden electric pump, and he switches it off at bedtime. One can't have everything one wants.

Since, too, one is a permanently unsatisfied worrier, one was fussing about unwanted phenomena. The bracken was invading again. A nasty weed; one must tell le père Poirier to come with his syringe and inject some drops of poison into the roots (hideously tough and rebellious) of these offences. Ferns of several sorts thrive in the shady moisture here. It is murder, yes, but bracken cannot be tolerated.

He bent over worrying about this rose. A climbing rose; in fact two, cunningly intermingled: simple, pretty, old-fashioned things: indeed a classic marriage. 'Nevada' and 'Marguerite Hilling', both sadly given to black spot. Not in good shape. One must ask Father Peartree his opinion, diagnosis. Which will be the more solemn and sententious because really he knows nothing about roses. They do not do well here and one always wonders why.

As he straightened up there came a sort of whop. Would perhaps a thop describe it better?

There are night-flying things. Come out with the owls. Moths for instance. Moths are pretty silent. Do not, definitely, go thop. There are also larger, harder, carapaced sort of things. He is no entomologist, calls them Junebugs even in October. To the best of his belief they are harmless. They might blunder into one's cheek, hard enough to make one rub it. They do not go thop; a short, dead, and yes, nasty sound.

Above all they do not, within one second, make a loud echoing and damnably sinister report. He didn't stop to define this at all. Be it bang, crack, whack or whatever, instinct takes over from literature. Brief, crouching low, running-very-fast, he was across the terrace and down the five-six steps to the house level. You could say jack-robinson, whoever he was, once twice, thrice, and he hadn't turned on the terrace lights; of course not and just-as-bloody-well into the bargain. That thop and that bang – horribly magnified by these damned trees – that's a rifle shot.

I write things down. Straight off, before they have time to cool. I write damn near anything down because the notebook is a writer's raw material. One can never know what one might want, for a book. One doesn't know when a book might suddenly start; taking one by surprise. Especially something like this, which is unusual: I hope it stays that way. I was interested in my own reactions. Dignified old gentleman running for a bus. London bus of course, leap on the platform and promptly drop dead. Or miss it and fall on the pavement; the Big Red One recedes mockingly. Noisy, pollutingly – one doesn't care, dead there on the roadway. This is no moment to be funny; that was a bullet and it barely missed me. My heart is now banging loudly, making more noise than a bus. I had the impression that the collar of my shirt was ripped, and had to look, to be sure I'd imagined it. That close.

I slammed the terrace door. I don't close the shutters as a rule before true nightfall, and then I often forget. This is a friendly house, and nothing in it worth stealing. We've never gone in for bars, bolts, and insurance companies.

Mr Charles is shaken, as well as greatly surprised at his mighty swiftness. Are there going to be more shots? Will one be frightened to put one's head out?

A drink, definitely. There is some single malt in the cellar, and he was not going down there to root about. Kitchen whisky and glad of it.

And pick up a pen. That will oblige the hand to stop trembling. Now – was there or wasn't there a second shot?

Or am I imagining that, too?

By tomorrow, I've no doubt, I'll be feeling extremely cross. Right now there's no room for anything but fright.

I've noticed this often enough. I'm old, damn it, and when I get an upset it gnaws at me, and it takes a night's sleep to put me to rights. Saying which I hope I do sleep. It doesn't alter the fact. I write rude letters and in the morning I tear them up. I don't feel humiliated by my fear. Somebody, possibly Napoleon, said one was no good for war after the age of thirty. Meaning bullets, quite true. That was a bullet, even if my shirt wasn't ripped. That whupping sound has been described often enough in fact as well as bad fiction. I am wondering about the second shot. We all think of our own reactions as fast, and driving the second car when the light goes green is a simple demonstration that they aren't. I curse the fellow in front for sleeping and no doubt the man behind curses me. I thought my reactions tumbling off the terrace pretty smart but feel sure that whoever it was had plenty of time for a second shot.

He missed; does that prove him incompetent? I wouldn't want to feel sure of that. From what I know of shooting, which is not a great deal, aiming downhill is tricky. A foreshortening effect; the slope from the woodland is steeper than it looks. One could look for signs whether anyone had got through the fence. Or rather, one will get the père Poirier to look. I can trust him.

These are notes. Obviously, writing things down has a calming effect, and an organising effect. But I am only following a life-time habit. A third reason occurs: if so be I get shot, there will be a police investigation. They'll find my notebook, which goes everywhere with me, and they'll read it, and I must do my best to make it useful reading.

Surely when I knew why I'd know who?

I have no idea. It ought to be obvious and perhaps it is. Now that I think a little, could be a dozen things and none perhaps more obvious than the others. Should I put it that I deserve no better? I am confused. This needs a lot more thought. One must try also to be logical, even if a lot of these people are extremely illogical, and will shooting at me solve their problems?

First things first. There's a man (?) outside there with a gun. Well he won't do anything tonight; I got away and now I've closed and barred all the shutters. Remains the attic, where I have an errand, for which I have to turn lights on. One has a view of this from up the hill. But the skylights are double glass, and my impression is that you couldn't shoot through those without a lot of distortion; your bullet would go awry for sure. It's ridiculous I know, but I'm still going to hunt for the armoury. Serves no purpose but will make me feel better? If no braver.

There's the twenty-two rifle: as I have often remarked, is there in France a single house without one? Formidable thing it is too; not a toy by any means and kills a great many people in the hands of French man, woman and child. I taught the children to shoot with it, never allowing them to be in front of it, never allowing them to use the magazine: never more than one cartridge at a time. I've never used it since and that's twenty years at the inside. It still stands in the corner of the bedroom where la mère Poirier treats it with respect when dusting: it will have gathered a great deal of dust. On the top shelf of the press behind hats is the cleaning rod, some soft rags and some three-in-one. Not all rusted I hope. No, just dirty; the boys put it away oiled.

No cheap job; a Walther, an excellent weapon, beautiful balance even for a ten-year-old. Why on earth has one kept it? One tells oneself there might be rats or marauding cats. There are the deer which have on occasion got in and chewed maple leaves. Do you remember the old Typhoo-Tea advert? – 'the tiny tip of the tender leaf'. Until Peartree mended and heightened the fence. I got very angry but never had the heart to shoot them. The worst ravages were made by a doe and two fawns. Stood there placidly gazing at me. I gazed back, trembling with violence and yelling. I never even thought of the gun. I do now, though. With the rags there's a half-used box of 'reduced-charge' ammo. Target stuff good only up to twenty-five metres. But a barely-used box of Russian high-speed, dangerous at several hundred. What kind of gun did my unknown friend have? A deer rifle, medium calibre Remington or Winchester, is common form around here.

I have really no idea what use this object can be. I have the vaguest possible notion of frightening someone off. Preposterous.

Nonetheless I have gone to rummage in the attic. Lots of fumbling about even if I have got rid of so much. It was still there. From forty years ago. Pot-Valiant bought that one day in Belgium. Wanted to have it, the way boys do. Never touched it since, it has never even been fired. Brand-new in the box; a simple – no, not foolproof – but very well made, like the Walther, nine-millimetre automatic pistol, Fabrique National de Herstal. Magazine separate so as not to weaken the spring. One box of twenty-five nice shiny copper – they're very old. Will they still go? Will I find out? Look, I'm not going to indulge in this going round in circles. Load the magazine, clip it in. Yes, I know how. Put on your corduroy jacket which has big flapped button-down pockets, and you put it in one of those. Leather button – yes, button it. I am aware that I feel the most awful fool. Tomorrow morning I'll think again about this.

Meanwhile; have you now got the courage to go down the road? To talk to Peartree?

It was eight o'clock. The time was important. First, the Peartrees would be finished with dinner. That much he knew, for it has happened that they say 'I'll be up after dinner' upon some small errand. It has meant that the meal was over, the dishes washed and the kitchen, where (as far as he is concerned) they have their being, has been tidied. That he knows also, for it has also happened that at this time he has visited them with some message as 'I'm off tomorrow morning' with whatever discussion of this fact might be called for. It would be bad manners, and thought so too, to intrude upon them at table. It would be bad manners to telephone. They are old-fashioned people (isn't he, also?) and like to be face to face with people they are talking to. He would phone of course from a distance, to say 'I'll be home tomorrow'. 'Home'? Perfectly good word; nothing wrong with it.

Eight o'clock is twenty hundred: the time of the 'sacred' evening news bulletin, the television's Vingt Heures. It means that nobody, at least in a French village, is on the road (and the fact, this minute, has some weight): they are all in front of their bright-lit box, and all with their mouths full. Not the Peartrees, who have not only no television, in a French countryside unheard of, but have and express forcibly an open contempt for this invention. 'For children. And nasty brats at that.' Thus, other people's conversation seems largely confined to last-night's-film: not theirs.

It would raise the question of what they do in the evening. They say to be sure that like their grandparents they go to bed with the hens. He has noticed them to be singularly well-informed about the world. The absence of television will itself account for that? They read to be sure the local paper, whose print gets larger as the news in it gets smaller, but that is to know who in the locality is dead.

He suspects that they read. People do, even now. Fewer, as he notices from his bank statements, but it goes on still. Might they read his own books, even? It would be bad manners to enquire and worse, in their view, to comment. What do they read? History? Biography? It is hard to tell with country people of their age. Their remarks are acute, and salty. They are intelligent, ordinarily so. Their schooling was short but thorough; scanty is not the word and neither is summary; they are both instructed and educated. Further they are highly articulate (the young are not). It remains something of an enigma.

He opened the door and for a moment he paused. The night was particularly black, with neither moon nor stars. He had turned out the lights; he wanted none behind him. He would in any case stand awhile to let his eyes grow used to darkness, always less black than it seems. When here, before going to bed, he does as a rule step outside and walk around the house. To take a sniff of the air. To see that there is nothing untoward: to let as it were the dog pee. So that he was used to blackness: cloudy nights are frequent. There are scattered houses further up the valley, but widely spaced. In the village are a few (feeble-minded) street lights but the Peartree house is itself well outside the village, and round a bend of the hill, and it is a hundred metres, perhaps two, down the road. To be out at night in the countryside is alarming. It could be perfectly still and one hears a scuffle; there might be a fox on the road. One hears footsteps and they turn out to be those of a deer. The trees talk among themselves. One could and would normally take a torch or a bike lamp: this, tonight, did not seem a good idea. He did, despite himself, feel pleased with the weight and shape and feel of the pistol in his pocket.

This is all the home he has. He was not there always, nor even very often. Two or three times a year, and he might stay a month or more; he did work there. Governments, meaning people who want forms filled in, for their comfortable livelihood depends upon it, get edgy if one isn't domiciled somewhere. They are contented if you give them stuff (doesn't have to be exact or even accurate; as long as it's a lot) to feed into their computer. They aren't much concerned at what comes out, for that is for other gentry to waste their time upon.

Now that he thought of it, this was the address given in reference books. So that anyone unknown to him, not too sure where to find him, would come looking for him here. There was a doorbell, mostly unanswered; a phone, still more frustrating for the intrusive. People try to sell one things. Quite often he rewinds the tape without listening. A phone ringing in an empty house is a temptation and perhaps a challenge to breakers-in; he has no poppers-in. Whatever the pest, the père Poirier will deal with it. He is paid for that, and enjoys it; has not all that much to do. One closes the eyes to still anxieties at the prospect of there being no père P. There might be no himself, either. Of the two, le Padre Pipi which is what la Mère calls him when in a bad mood, is the more solid. Which means nothing; it never does.

Pa Peartree, irresistible name for one good with gardens, is retired on a small pension, happy with John's contribution to ends-of-the-month the year round. Tall dignified man, wears a beret (which few do nowadays) of immeasurable antiquity; never seen without it; could be bald as an egg but the features go somehow with straight fine grey hair. There is generally a flavour of pastis about him, but not showing in his eyes or nose. One may believe it is kept under strict control by Ma Peartree, a rangy rawboned woman with a powerful stride and feet to match, and who has been pretty. Still is, I suppose, since unlike most countryfolk of her generation (and his own) she has good teeth.

There are also Poirier dogs, which live in a woodshed between the two properties. They are well trained but ferocious; cannot be handled by anyone else; nor would they accept food but from their masters. They know him, and do not bark. They are loosed night and morning for half an hour, and scour around. It occurs to him that no one would get closer than the woodland outskirts without their setting up a racket: there is good protection there.

Like all French people anywhere they hate persons in the house. They are free of his own, so that they are formally polite. Chair offered, a 'little glass'; he is 'always welcome'.

"Sorry to be dropping in" (faces of 'no no') "wished only to know whether you had noticed any strangers, hanging about at all." He felt embarrassed by his own terror and suppressed telling him of the shot. "Would have remarked," said Peartree with perfect certainty; the English word 'remarkable' belongs to this pattern. If the Peartrees hadn't, the dogs would. A suspicious watchfulness is ingrained in this people. Not long ago a parcel service had appeared (proofs, for correction, from a publisher) insisting naturally on a signature for delivery, given in his absence by Pa Peartree after a good long look.

'Red Fiat wagon,' he had reported, 'didn't get the number but registered in the Seine-Maritime.' When you

take a responsibility for others . . . "No." But think about it.
"No."

"Thought maybe some loiterer."

"But will keep the eye open," offered Marie-Madeleine
briskly.

Whether he is home or not she comes once a week 'to
do the house', accounting for every penny spent on clean-
ing materials, striding on her long legs, flinging open
windows to air. He wouldn't even know her name but for
Peartree (when in a bad mood) spitefully whistling

>*'Marie-Madeleine a*
>*Une petite chose en laine,*
>*Marie-Madeleine a*
>*Un petit garçon.'*

Brazen aspersion upon her morals that ruffles the
respectable lady's feathers. In an unusually good frame of
mind, when working, he will whistle the song about the
little girl who was teased by the fishermen and got sadly
vexed about it.

>*'A la pêche-e de moules-e*
>*Je ne veux plus aller, Maman.'*

It is likely that neither of them has ever seen the sea.
They are French in ways that have become a rarity. A clean-
liness of spirit; he'd no more covet his neighbour's wife
than steal from a supermarket, because meanness isn't in
him. Her – the moon would turn to cheese, she'd cut a
slice and eat it too, first. While the State! The Church!
Either will give a look – as though you suggested they swallow a dirty dishclout. A proud, and humble scepticism that
in others is shallow, cynical and egoist. A President is only

a mayor in a palace and whatever the others call themselves it's only greed and greasy vainglory. In agglomeration the State is a bureaucracy whose arrogant lethargy is checked only by built-in imbecility. Their love is given to the poor; the pursued and the persecuted; the lost, and the hopeless. The afflicted-by-God (whose purposes are unknown to us); this can cover a great deal, is mysteriously more widespread among Arabs or Jews, can never quite make out at what point Allah and Jehovah formed a disagreement.

Both Peartrees have also all the usual French targets for an inimical attitude: Foreigners, Blacks, Parisiens; Curés, Officials, Tourists.

How does he himself escape hanging?

I felt better, going back up the hill. A baddish moment there only where the house wall forms a deeper shadow upon the darkness; the hand once unclenched from the pistol butt was, distinctly, sweaty. Turn key, push bolts; both could do with a drop of the three-in-one and so could wrists and elbows. Shoulders knees and ankles too; take a bath in the stuff why don't you? Total illogical anxiety then about that stupid ammunition. Went into the second cellar which is full of junk (the first is the wine-cellar; nothing very grand but deserving of respect) and found a piece of insulating material, is its silly name expanded-polystyrene, then no sillier than I feel. Prop it up, stand five metres off. Took two pops, satisfying bang, in the cellar made my ears ring for a good five minutes. Two holes quite small and comfortingly close together, hold it fairly low because a nine-mill tends to jump and will throw high; don't aim but hold banger naturally like extension of own hand; as though pointing forefinger. Remove poly-thing. Shots knocked off a lot of saltpetre and took a nice clean chip off stone. Went upstairs, ejected magazine, pulled-through-banger, cleaned and reloaded. Felt lots better. The night air outside, ever since the twilight has made me think of childhood, of the most purely wonderful twilight an English child can know.

Do children still sing?

> *'Please to remember*
> *The Fifth of November'?*

One can't surely ask 'Fifty Pee for the guy, Mister'; apart from sounding so silly it has no rhythm. I'm bleeding internally, Mister, since of all my English childhood this has been among the most painful of losses. Light the blue touchpaper, and stand well back. Preferable to the nine-millimetre (leaving the pistol at bedside).

John did not sleep well; fever-frets at three in the morning. The bad time, said Kipling, when the cattle wake for a little. Do they? It makes an effective phrase, which a writer applauds. Mr K was at his best, he tells us, around five, and with a south-west wind blowing. But not – as now – if he shot upright, hearing 'a funny noise'.

I am a rogue and peasant slave. The word got me out of bed, a good word trivialised. Roguish little fellow. Etymologies are my bread and butter, and dictionaries a substitute for sleep.

Concise Oxford, rarely much use. 'Idle vagrant' – a concise description of oneself. 'The beast driven apart from the herd, of savage temper' – likewise. Etymology dubious: the lazy buggers.

The 'Petit Robert' is a great deal better, as usual. 13th cent. Scandinavian – 'arrogant'. Adjective, contemptuous or cutting; rude. This, John, is also close to the target. Let's have a try at Shorter Oxford.

A bit pathetic this; the elderly gentleman thus mustily employed. Well, what would you do, if you couldn't sleep; consequence of being shot at? Hillyards' Flower Catalogue is also a reliable aid.

Shorter is a little help; nothing flamboyant. Possibly the root is the Latin 'rogare', to ask or to beg. Not bad: Shakespeare's Autolycus or Mr John Charles, both sturdy beggars. Pedlars. Village story-tellers, chatting-up the probably neglected, doubtless sexually-deprived village housewife. A perfectly accurate description of the average lending-library novelist. Not at all inapposite.

Rogue – adjective. Uncontrolled, undisciplined – irresponsible. Hum. One wondered why the Scandinavian meaning had got into French and not into English. Into Scottish, perhaps? And had one made any real headway?

But this was surely how the word had got into his three-in-the-morning subconscious. Idle vagrant, well and good. But the solitary beast of savage temper? One did recall that 'Rogue Male' – wonderful title, respectable writer – the English gentleman, a big-game hunter out of the Rider Haggard stable, took a pot at Hitler. Splendid stuff. Motivation, he has lost his wife, suppressed (that is rather obscure) by the tyrant. Alas, the admirable Mr Household's imagination had galloped away with him and it all went downhill after that wonderful start; into childhood memories of Dorset countryside. Were there any clues here for himself?

His wife to be sure had been German, and about her beginnings had hung a bit of the usual murky National Socialist dirt. Born under a cloud, you might say. She'd had nothing to do with the Tyrant. Nor had she been suppressed. After thirty years of marriage she had left him. Prosaic. Nothing there.

Who had shot at him? Above all, why? It wouldn't be any

English gentleman either. Had he even been shot at – seriously? Yes. It was Not his imagination.

One will have to have a word with Pa Peartree about this. There is no sense in pretending it didn't happen.

"Monsieur Poirier, good morning. Yes, not bad, is it? Bit of mist. Rather dewy. Still, once the sun gets through. That, in fact, I wanted a word. You might have noticed, last night I might have appeared a bit pent. Fact is, somebody took a pop at me with a rifle. I don't think there's any way one could write it off as accident."

Straightfaced, if anything stolid, le père Poirier did admit he had noticed that, well, something seemed to have upset you. Not his place to make any comment. La bourgeoise (one of his names for his wife) had been a bit taken-aback.

Quite so. One will adopt the cool and detached approach. Not in the least a 'ton rogue'. Not the moment to be cutting, contemptuous, and certainly not arrogant.

"I'm bound to take it seriously. However dotty. No wish to go to the gendarmerie or anything like that. One would want to know more first. Purely factual. Occurred to me, all this dew, might be footprints, whatever, broken bushes, up there by the fence. I wondered whether perhaps you might like to take a look, by daylight."

Yes indeed. This is a methodical man, meticulous in all he does. A plumb line, a spirit level. Even if driving a post into the ground. That's the way he goes about it.

"Mind my asking, whereabouts you were? Might find a bullet. And up the hill there, if it ejected normally, might find a cartridge case." And when he says he'll have a butchers, he'll be very thorough indeed. When observed, mounting the field, he had a dog with him, and a gun slung on his shoulder.

"Some coffee?" Merci in French means no.

"Sure thing, Monsieur Charles. Bullet hit the rock, where you were standing. Flattened, nothing to make of that. Only had to work out the trajectory then. Made himself like a nest in the long grass. No proper footprints; smeared like, flattened. Didn't try to get through the fence; would have been a job if I do say so. Could have cut the wire, acourse, might have thought it alarmed – that might be an idea, wouldn't be all that hard. Don't want a chap creeping up on one. That's not any dotty, that was planned, to waylay you, like. Course, if you don't want any gendarmes . . . They're not likely to find anything more than me, if I do say so. Went away through the wood. Had the dog follow that, but no distance. Rained, since." Peartree launched into a lengthy description of the sort of technical device he relishes; an alarm based on some concealed tripwire, low voltage electric current, something similar to the light mobile barrier farmers use to pen a few sheep, keep them from straying. But one doesn't regret taking him into confidence. A careful man, reliable and discreet.

This is psychobabble. I'm aware that I'm still feeling shock, and suffering from it. One difficulty is that I don't know where to begin. Courage? – I have as much as the next man; it's been put to the test a few times. Physical courage is only one sort. One thinks of Rabin, urged by his security people to wear a bullet-proof jacket; refusing, saying 'Ridiculous'. Wasn't the real courage the telling himself he'd been wrong, after a stubborn lifetime of zapping Arabs? Or De Gaulle, climbing out of the bullet-scarred flat-tyred Citroën saying 'Lousy shots'; one expects a general to have this kind of courage. But I am not even a Corsican municipal councillor; I don't go about expecting people to pot at me from the street corner.

Is it even serious? One can imagine somebody anxious to give me a good fright. A warning, a deliberate close-shave. The miss is neater, smarter than the zap; a way of saying 'We could just as easily have knocked your stupid head off. Reading us loud and clear, are you?' Or was it some National Front hooligan getting a good giggle out of seeing me skip?

I can make a little list. There could be a dozen – call them groups – who could be tickled by this notion of frightening me with false fire: keep the real fire for when it's needed.

I am not a journalist. Like any writer I've done journalism in my time. Investigative; I have done a few pieces to shed a sharp light on people who prefer to stay in the shade, but as a rule I haven't tried to compete with the real ones, whose job it is. A few years back in Sarajevo (lot of people insisting we all wore bullet-proof jackets) I did some writing which upset United Nations officers as well as Serbs, keeping my admiration and respect for the men and women, reporters, photographers, taking far greater risks than I ever did: a large number left their skin there-about. I have contributed to the discomfort of politicians, right here in France. Elsewhere too in Europe. And nowadays very many people think of physical violence first, as an answer to whatever has bitten them.

But this is so vague. No direct link in causality. There are plenty of people around who would get this angry at a dint put in their household gods (the car, in France; touch my car and you injure me deep in my deepest sensitivities). They'll jump out after some trivial bump and they've a gun in their hand . . . You know then where you stand. And why.

Oddly enough, I think the père Poirier might be on the right lines. Need an alarm system, a tripwire. Not literally but something to draw this oddity on, or is it out? Oddity, it's how I think of him, could be a her I suppose, but lying up there with a rifle doesn't seem like a woman's way of doing things. So let's call him Oddity.

Something's beginning to take shape here. What perseverance would be shown? People get mad enough to shoot one, knife one, throw a bomb at one, charge one with a chain saw; half an hour later they'll have thought better of it. How cool-blooded is this? What planning goes to it?

I'm not going to hang about here wondering when he'll take another pop at me. People, it's well enough established, tend to stick to the same method in their madness. One sees it in suicides; if they've already tried gunshots they won't of a sudden think of turning on the gas. Nor do I fancy walking about waiting to be shot at. I'm not a general. I may be average brave, I'm also average cowardly.

So leave. That could be thought quite normal: I do leave and often very suddenly. I've work to do here, but it can wait. Go somewhere, take a varied kind of rhythm, sometimes abrupt and as often leisurely. See whether anyone follows.

Where would one go? This seems quite easy too. Draw Oddity, assuming he comes along, into a one-way street, a bag or pocket where I would stand a good chance of recognising, maybe identifying, ideally isolating him. In theory at least, pull him up a blind alley, turn round and walk up to him and ask what the hell do you think you're playing at. Somewhere small and simple, a village, where a stranger is at once noticed.

Yes but one mustn't assume he's a perfect imbecile. There has to be a feint, but there must also be a logical explanation for my own behaviour, which he would accept as probable. The mistake, and the fatal weakness, in the

'Rogue Male' story was that this active and intelligent man would go and bury himself in a cave in the wilds of Dorset. Not even noticing that he was putting himself up the blind alley, a stupid rabbit waiting for the ferret. Oddity must assume that I have a purpose in going there; a plainly obvious way out. Eccentric perhaps, but I'm known to be an eccentric man. It has to make sense to him, and to his reading of me.

After puzzling for a hour or two over maps, I think I have an acceptable answer. I'll go right across France (and quick-quick-slow, to see what accompaniment there might be) into Finisterre.

France is a largish place, by European standards. If one is used to small crowded countries, like Holland or England, it can appear enormous. It can also appear oddly empty, so that one could quite readily believe oneself in some country not on the way to anywhere; Spain say, or Sweden. There are not those disconcerting huge numbers of people which in Germany strike the senses of the voyager, all so busy, so damnably active and apparently intent on going somewhere else. For a country bang in the centre of Western Europe, with frontiers leading to everywhere else, it is strangely static. One could say sleepy, backward. Off the main lines of communication (and even often on them) one wouldn't be far wrong.

To be sure, there are historic reasons for this. Every road leads to Paris. Betimes one can believe that everyone in France has gone to Paris and stayed there; once there it is all too easy to believe that the rest of France doesn't exist: notoriously this is the firm conviction of everyone who lives and works there. There is Lille, yes, and Lyon; large, modern, bustling cities which the Parisian (with an effort) can call to mind. Everywhere else, and this includes famous and important historic capitals of large and wealthy regions, is a nowhere. Only the native-born, who have lived their entire life in Toulouse or Bordeaux, could believe themselves somewhere, and then with much effort. There is nowhere in France a Hamburg or a Munich. Did one hear someone mention Marseille? True, they make there a great noise because it's full (in more or less equal ratio) of Arabs, gangsters, and Corsicans: go there and you will find a provincial backwater.

Discount all this as Parisian vanity and there is still a lot of truth in it. Try out Rennes or Nancy of a Sunday evening, Dijon or Rouen. They have been capital cities in their day.

Mr Charles is used to all this; he has lived in France for many years. These people have a streak of genius, seen in their engineering, and they cling to bygone grandeurs, nostalgia for the Sun King. The widening rupture makes them schizophrenic. No wonder that they eat so many pills to calm them down.

John is seventy, placid about it; that's not old by today's measurement. Old enough to have seen a lot, travelled a bit. A cosmopolitan, at home pretty much anywhere, if the climate's temperate. He's not easily bothered, by Events. He's surprised now, by this upheaval, for he hadn't thought there was anything left to be frightened by.

And now – yes, he feels fear. Enjoying it, too. At this age the heart, the emotions, are familiar companions. Turbulent at times still. Boring, mostly, since this is an age when the arteries begin to fail, or your prostate starts giving trouble. There isn't much to be excited by. Now he is pleased to find himself excited. A thunderbolt arrives? Let us confront this thunderbolt.

He quite likes his plan, but there are complications. Crossing France, now that's a bore. Take a plane? If on the way to Los Angeles one hasn't a lot of choice; here one has plenty. Further, a plane is too rigid, too obvious, too easily traced. Enter the toothpaste tube and get squeezed out at the far end. You get put on the computer, which any busybody can gawk at. No planes.

There are trains though, even today. He has always loved trains. They have the infernal habit of going to Paris and stopping there. And once on a train you are stuck with it. Anybody can walk about observing you. Disguised as a nun your boots will betray you, and there's luggage to cart about.

Whereas with the car . . . at least he wouldn't be wearing a ring in his nose. It leaves a trail, it can be followed, but there's a freedom of movement, one slides into bypaths, one doubles back, one will be cunning.

Why? What is there to be cunning about? Aren't you getting paranoid, being buffaloed? Outside the stupid accident, I don't believe in that, and the deliberate attempt at murder, I've trouble with that, too, there's a big area in between.

Grey area; a plan to frighten him, upset his nerve. Destabilise; piece of ignorant jargon, but bring about a state of worry and tension. What for, what's the point? It's a petty world; don't underestimate small spiteful meanness. Envy, a trivial grievance cherished and magnified. A lot of crime is like this. Small, secretive, disgusting crimes. They don't get into the paper; people know, but say nothing. The police may know, and have their reasons for preferring not to. A pillow put over Granny's face; there are no proofs. Doesn't have to be murder. An old friend, or partner, manoeuvred out of his job. A reputation blackened, a wife seduced, a witness suborned, some children perverted. There are no statistics about this sort of crime, and one can become a victim without even knowing it. I have seen, known, a lot, over the years.

Or a warning? To let something alone, to forget? What?

One thing they all have in common; that if caught they can whine. 'But I meant no harm; I only wanted to give him a fright.' And the young – they can be the most frightening of all. An act of extreme violence and for no reason. It is enough that they think it funny.

Travelling, for the most part unhurried, in a mostly northwesterly direction, he could put on carefree airs. This was all on the whole agreeable, the way it ought to be for an elderly gentleman in sound health, no money worries, who has decided to lay care aside, leave any little domestic difficulties behind. 'Read, and go south for the winter' – Eliot, was it? A damned smug remark, but one could sympathise.

The car is an Audi, not grand but adequate to the needs and circs. of said gent; nothing flashy (asking to be stolen) but no tin can either, the reliable and respectable upper end of the Volkswagen engineering works. A pale colour, to be visible at twilight, but nothing that will show the dirt. Comfortable, efficient, silent. A prudent car, and prudent is what he feels. On the back shelf are a number of maps and guides to fleshpots: one should be comfortable at night, after eating well, and a midday pause should encompass a good walk, with something of interest to look at, and a small meal (but not just hamburger either). It was a day or two before he became disgusted with his horrible smugness.

He felt, by now, pretty sure he was not being followed. When he came upon an autoroute he had driven fast, and turned off it suddenly. He had done abrupt stops and illogical reversals; had plunged into tangles and made wide swerves away from any foreseeable path of pattern: he was confident he would have spotted anyone taking an interest. He had poked for reactions; a clever-little-dick would have been tempted or provoked out of hiding.

To the Peartrees he had said only that he had some business calling him away; they were used to this. Pa had rather relished a few ingenious ideas; all set indeed to phone up Fichet (specialist in locks, safes and the like) for a nice chat about burglar alarms. He had dismissed this; poopoo, some beersodden boy, the type that defaces tombstones. Alarms are poppycock, there's nothing in the house worth stealing – which was perfectly true. Vandalism would be revolting but one had rather more faith in the dogs than in Fichet: give him a lot of keys he'd mislay them or forget what they were for, and there was truth in that, too.

Now there was a very pleasant country hotel, soft-treading, soft-spoken, a lot of felt underlay to the personnel as well as the carpets, and judging by the menu a good ambitious cook; shellfish, large fish, plenty of seaweed. One was overlooking Quiberon Bay and the brisk walk along the littoral would be undertaken. The tide was out; there were pungent smells but not of drains. There was a magnificent evening cloudscape after the manner of Doré, of piled cumulus and brilliant oblique spears of sunlight. This artist – one would not say just illustrator – had been of much moment in his childhood. Godparents with a belief in solid cultural presents; the massive volumes of *Quixote* and *Paradise Lost*. Which was here, surely, and one would certainly expect to see angels – or perhaps Satan, thinking. One could see a long way, and there was nobody there at all. A dinghy or two, moored, empty.

Instead there were birds. Oyster-catchers walked about, curlews cried with mournful notes; that is to say he thought they were curlews but perhaps they were whippoorwills – but as long as they were delightful to the ear . . . Also a great many ducks, which sat and bobbed about on the water; mallard, teal? Towards sunset would there be flights, migrating, or was it too early, not cold enough yet for geese? A seagull or two, perching on an old post, waiting to be painted and sold as Regional Art to tourists. It was time to stop being lazy, pleased with oneself, cooked – casseroled, smothered in his own juice and fat, served up in an earthenware pot (regional art) to be eaten by himself with relish. Enough of this cannibalistic autosatisfaction.

He didn't believe that he had been shot at by accident. The drunken teenager would do for the Peartrees but not for him. What was he doing here? This was pointless, as well as paradise lost. Running away is easy. There would come the moment when he had to go back. Why would anyone bother to follow him, here? That would be senseless, hysterical, in a pattern with his own behaviour.

He'd overestimated his own attractions, hadn't he. Had then gone to enormous trouble to lose anyone who did feel interested enough to . . .

He looked at the seagull, which looked back at him, the way they do, nasty beasts, with contempt. He was no good to eat, or not yet.

"You are a great fool," he told himself. It didn't say, "I quite agree." Shit, instead; laconic, comes to the same thing.

By midday of the following, having reached the famous blind pocket into which he had designed to draw a pursuer, he was in doubt again. Who's in the pocket then – him or me? The last hundred kilometres, there seemed to have been a blue car, as though shepherding, from some distance back. Hadn't there been a blue car at the outset just like that, same make and similar behaviour? Look, it is a common make, and a commonplace colour.

Roscoff is a small village on the seaward edge of Finisterre. It has no peculiarities; the usual granite huddle, a perhaps unusually ugly church, a fishing harbour, convalescent homes doing seawater therapy, full of oldies on crutches because of hip-replacements – and a floating population of Brits, for round the corner there's a ferry port with a link to Plymouth, heavily loaded with the never-ending local cauliflower. This had been the purpose of his long-winded scheme: it is the deadest of dead ends, leading nowhere save over-the-sea-to-Skye.

Having come all this way, so elaborately, one must not get faint-hearted. This meant a zealous feint to the ferry terminal, looking like a man reserving tickets, and hanging about in the dorp until sailing time, keenly observant of attendant Oddities, ready to confront and confound. Mister Charles has friends in the west of England, whom he hasn't seen for some years, and why not Wales too while one's at it?

A heartening aspect is that it's a remarkably fine day. 'La Mer, la mer, toujours recommencée': he has no great opinion of Valéry and Brittany is boring but Sète still more so. A true northerner, he loves these Finisterre seas. He lunched in the harbour front café which had a glassed-in terrace and a good view of passers-by; ate a fresh but grandfatherly crab, overdoing the mayonnaise somewhat. The yacht harbour dries out at low tide. People aren't sailing much, this late in the year. The fishing industry was somnolent too, not to say stagnant. Two or three touristy old salts in weather-beaten caps pretended to be busy with cordage and bait, an excuse for sitting in the warm sunshine. Mayonnaise provided reasons for walking in the sunshine. There were quite a lot of Brits with the same idea, some like himself, elderly Brits who had come a long way from the south and arrived too early for fear of arriving late. Himself is always an hour early in airport departure lounges, gets peppery at the wait which is his own fault.

Brits can be recognised easily through the odd knobbly faces, the peculiar clothes. Getting on in life, they have addictions to strange hats and walking sticks. One such sat in the café (ate fish and chips, punished a bottle of Muscadet), caught his notice for refusing despite the warmth to take off the Burberry (he had left his own in the car): an English certainty that it IS going to rain. And an Irish tweed cap, rather a nice one. And a stick, propped awkwardly against a chair, it kept falling down, as though having made similar inroads upon the local plonk.

On the far side of the fishing boats is a jetty, little but quite long, pottering out to sea in aimless fashion so that on wonders what on earth it is for. It ends in a little light, probably described in the *Channel Pilot* as 'misleading', and two or three more old-salts fishing and never catching anything. An approved after-mayonnaise pastime is to walk out along this. In the sea are a lot of weedy rocks, some shallow pools of bright emerald, the ruinous foundations of ancient 'viviers' where people used to keep live lobsters, a few wading birds which stalk about catching things, a view of the Ile de Batz and the little ferries which bring tourists there. And on the ragged concrete walkway there is a lot of dogshit because this post-prandial stroll is found healthful by all, which includes the dogs. After that everything happened very fast.

Shot, so quick, so clean an ending? Not invariably. Sleepy from sun, crab, mayonnaise (he dislikes the local plonk) he saw nothing at all. Noticed nothing save that whoever got shot it wasn't him. Familiar human condition; everything has happened and nobody knows anything, quite as usual.

"No, I wasn't looking."

"I saw everything." But 'How little we know' as Lauren Bacall intoned sexily, looking over her shoulder. The gendarmerie of course are only too familiar with this line.

"It was a Déséquilibré." This lovely word is frequent in French conversation: equilibrium was a quality prized in life here, once upon a time.

"Monsieur, it was the Arabs."

"Madame, don't talk to me about Arabs, I'm that terrified of them."

Having seen absolutely nothing, much like Sir Bedivere thinking it a pity to throw away that good sword, he stayed still and kept quiet. One might learn something from eavesdropping, unlikely as it seemed.

"Louis, did you see an Arab?"

"Can't say I did." One could hardly think of anywhere in France where one would be less likely to see Arabs.

"One will have to phone the gendarmerie."

"The gendarmerie will, there is no doubt, be needed." An abiding characteristic of French conversation is the sententious platitude delivered in formal language.

"It seems to me that the first necessity will be a doctor." Tautologies likewise.

"Has that matter been taken in hand? The telephone . . ."

"The harbourmaster's office."

"Harbourmaster, bonjour, the ferry booking office." Nobody budged, unwilling to lose a second of a dream.

"Louis, what d'you make of this?"

"Il souffre, le pauvre. Gunshot wounds, I can speak with experience, I remember that in the war –"

"Madame, it is atrocious. I cannot see and remain indifferent."

31

"It has come to this, Madame. Honest citizens are assassinated on the street by Arabs and the government does nothing to protect us."

"It is certain, that it was Arabs?"

"Louis saw an Arab, as clearly as I see you."

"Where is this doctor? They sit in comfort, drinking coffee, disliking to be disarranged."

"The ambulance does not contain doctors. In Paris, yes. But this is not Paris."

"Louis, putting the jacket under his head, is that a good idea? He should the least possible be disarranged."

"Where there is loss of blood it should be arrested."

"Don't tell me about gunshot wounds, I have reason to be considered an expert."

"Louis, we have here a situation that requires clearness of thought."

"Madame, is it not scandalous that such things of our days can be thought possible?"

"Madame, I do not cease from repeating that as long as Arabs walk with impunity upon our streets –"

"Taking the bread from our mouths –"

"They have six, eight, ten children, the government pays them to reproduce comme les lapins."

"And how is it that the rabbits become a rarity while the Arabs are ever more frequent, tell me."

"Madame, it is because we have disregarded the words spoken by the Blessed Virgin to the children of Fatima."

"Madame, it is the truth, Sainte Anne d'Auray pray for us all."

"Here at last is this ambulance."

"We must await the gendarmerie. They will not long delay. The eye-witness testimony is of the most urgent importance."

"That's another crowd never there when you want them."

"We must wait, Madame, to fulfil our civic obligations."

"Madame, it is true. How else shall these Arabs be brought to justice?"

"Without our civic sense, there would be no more justice in France."

"Louis, il était comment, l'Arabe?"

"J'ai pas vu d'Arabe, moi."

"He is in a bad way, le pauvre monsieur."

"Monsieur, the ambulance man, will he live?"

"If you get out from under foot, maybe."

"Louis, it is your duty to wait for the gendarmerie."

"Yes, fuckitt, and then I miss the tide."

"Louis, there can be no doubt nor hesitation."

"My duty and the gendarmerie both, I sodomise in series."

"Don't talk like that, Louis, it brings bad luck."

"Madame, it is as God disposes of our poor lives and wills."

"Madame, it is undeniable."

The gendarmerie isn't green, and it isn't cabbage-looking either, which in a countryside where the cabbages stretch limitless to the horizon (when they aren't artichokes) is saying a good deal. Most of the afternoon strollers had sloped off: the smallish group remaining was filtered without too much ado. A flip of a salute and, "Papers."

Mr Charles produced his passport.

"English? Having a walk? See anything?" No more than the truth, so far, if a little less. "Catching the boat?"

"I hope so." The gendarme looked at him. Plainly shocked, frightened, bells still chiming thirteen. Gave him his passport back and said, "On your way." Well, it wasn't any more than the truth. Authority turned to a group of old men and bloodthirsty small boys and uttered the classic, "Circulez, y a rien à voir." Quite so and he made tracks, horribly aware of the nine millimetre pistol in his pocket. They'd love that!

They'd give short shrift to the pious females and their Arabs. They'd concentrate upon the gunshot expert, the sort of elderly fusspot ever-ready to give himself airs of importance. Upon Louis; they'd know all about Louis, who had a net whose mesh was smaller than permitted by Community regulations, probably a smuggler and an illegal distiller, and was quite often drunk-and-disorderly late at night ('Tapage nocturne'). Much good might it do them; he had hung around long enough to be sure that nobody knew anything.

Now there were four; a gendarmerie officer and a one-striper in a small Peugeot. Now they'd get busy with pieces of chalk and measuring tapes. It had sounded – could one tell, out there, practically at sea? – like a medium calibre, perhaps a seven sixty-five (smaller than this huge thing in his pocket). If an automatic, they might find spent cartridge cases. Had there been two shots or three? Had they been from the front or from the back? He hoped the poor chap would survive: depended what they hit, inside, but close up like that it would be a toss-up and one couldn't help thinking that it should have been him.

The officer will make the local clinic his next stop. Get the news, and if they haven't exited, recover the bullets. The poor chap has a chance. It will be a well-equipped surgical clinic and not just hip replacements: they will have people competent in internal abdominal work. Were it him, and assuming he were anyway lucid, he'd be telling himself that from here to Paris or to London they'd be no better. Which is, he supposes, one consolation.

I can tell you, on the best possible authority, I like nigh to fucking shit. Lookitt, fellow ten paces in front of me, happens to be dressed the same as me, is English – you've the cap, the stick, the sort of walk. The features. I don't know, might have some resemblance. What to say, 'the Arab' melted into the landscape molto-pronto, can't buttonhole him to ask, Have you seen me before, how were you sure it was Me? Was this some hired hand, who got things confused? Makes that much more confusion in my mind too. He had to get out of here fast and did he think oh fuck, I've got the wrong one? I better get my own ass out of here speedy, because a dim gendarme might be bright and notice that I looked almost identical. They'll check everyone getting on the boat, that is for sure. I'd say I was all right with the car, in the momentary flurry. Gendarmerie will be looking at Brits. I showed my English passport, did not come clanking out with my French resident identity card, nor my French driving licence: if they look, it'll be for a Brit car and not French-registered wheels.

The fellow's miles away by now; Morlaix and beyond, could be in Rennes: once there, for awhile I'd feel I was clear.

The gendarme lieutenant will concentrate on the victim, poor bugger. If conscious, if lucid; they'll be interrogating poor bloody Michael Alan Rigby from Leicester and he'll wish to fucking heaven he'd stayed there; won't come here again in a hurry, here's where dotty Arabs take a pot at you, thought you were the one the Ayatollah said waste that infidel and you'll go straight to Heaven.

They'll find nothing. There will be a long unreadably wooden report in quintuplicate, one of which will go to the C.I.D. in Leicester, and the local branch of Barclays Bank is going to do some worrying too; what has our blameless Mr Rigby been up to?

But get out of here, before somebody notices you and

Mr Rigby are twins. I feel, I feel – I don't know what I feel. I'm friendly with pretty near any corner of Europe, but I don't think I'll ever want to see Brittany again.

The car was parked in front of that church, where it would be nice and obvious. Was that what I wanted? I don't know what I wanted. I feel panicked, and this is a sad state of affairs for an elderly gentleman commanding – I don't think that's the word and neither is 'deserving' – respect (mostly just for having been around a good many years) in literary circles: you can add a lot of other people's literary circles, and they add up to a life which isn't a bed of pain. I ought to be allowed – I should think – to slip by easy stages into dignified retirement. Rather like some eminent professor, whose qualities of genuine scholarship and admitted brilliance in his own field have brought him to a distinguished Chair, an acknowledged worldwide authority upon some mighty figure, Jane Austen say, or Conrad. After annoying several generations of students, having for years provoked all his contemporaries into rage, bored the public with a long list of books, collected honorary Doctorates from twenty universities and lectured in Japan, withdrawal is effected to an architecturally impeccable manor in Oxfordshire (velvet lawns and a Gothic library), there to write long letters to *The Times Literary Supplement* and make occasional rumbustious appearances on television. It is important to be noisily and even rabidly patriotic, fairly far to the right politically (to have advised the Prime Minister upon a number subjects about which both of you know nothing is a help) and to have a cellarful of excellent claret.

I am none of these things, which is why I am badly rattled, right now driving at the extreme of legal speed in an unexpected direction (Normandy; what the hell am I doing in Normandy?). I am concentrating hard upon the road, which is why I can let my mind sideslip this way.

Kipling wrote a wonderful, difficult and decidedly odd story called 'Dayspring Mishandled' about such a figure, the world's authority (quite genuine) upon Chaucer and dignified by his monarch into Sir Alured Castorley. He is of course the most appalling shit. Most people are, and I am as contemptible as most of them. One is right to think so, wrong to plan an extremely elaborate literary and personal revenge upon Sir Alured, as Manallace does.

It is right to believe that such people deserve all they get. One can reckon with certainty upon a life of conspiracy and be fairly sure that arrival was reached by foul means rather than well-developed skills of self-advertisement. Traces of this can survive in public. Maugham wrote a vicious book about Hugh Walpole, but Willie was a nasty man. One never heard that Galsworthy was a nasty man; said to have been both kind and generous. Got a Nobel Prize for being a mediocrity but that happens often. Luck can play a tremendous role; the public is very odd. Jack Priestley wrote some dull books and became a mighty saint apparently on account of a pipe and a Yorkshire accent. At any given moment one has a whole benchful of literary bishops, all quite unreadable.

I shouldn't be talking like this. I'm not jealous of anybody that I can think of. Sell fifteen thousand copies and it's a comfortable independence: more than that and the price to pay gets steeper, smartish. Nobody ought to be jealous of me, really. Nonetheless there have always been a good few Ayatollahs laying for me, as a declared enemy to religion. And in other countries there are saints, of several persuasions, who have taken quite a sharp dislike for me as the Professor of Comparative Literature, who whenever a book of mine appears go to quite unusual trouble to ensure that I get pissed on.

Take France, simply as the country closest home. Now

Graham, who lived for reasons best known to him in a small flat in Antibes, got into trouble with the municipality of Nice; it wasn't all to do with his current mistress. The Mayor of Nice was a well-known if then uncondemned (hardly denounced when Graham took him on) crook on a large scale. Greene got some impressive evidence together, deployed it with his accustomed talent (no better writer alive and good at polemics too); and the results were surprising. Literary columns in respectable newspapers took on cutting phrases: admiration for admitted, if perhaps lightweight, fictional gifts, satire, English humour, etc., had doubtless gone to Mr Greene's head. He had chosen to push his nose into matters which did not in the least concern him. His adulteries should be kept in the bedroom and his well-known Secret Service connections elsewhere: the Cote d'Azur is not Greeneland. A lot of rhetorical banging on the table; Blimey.

One might dare say that there are some shady characters in Nice; that a few of these thought seriously about Molotov cocktails and even a gun or two; thought better of that when told that the subject of these affections is a pretty famous figure, you know, and not just in Perfidious Albion neither.

Now I'm not a famous figure, nor anything near it. But perhaps that's why somebody could decide I'd be no loss to the world. I don't know who; there are several possibilities, some noted on my little list but there could be more I haven't thought of and don't even know about.

I'm close on Caen. I could go on with the autoroute Rouenward, Parisward. But I want a moment to think. I'll get accused, and I'll be the accuser, of being inward-looking; abnormally, and pathologically interested in my own digestive processes. I suspect that being shot at, and seeing a man shot in my place, does have this effect. One is reminded of Dr Johnson's dictum, over quoted until it became threadbare, but penetrating at the time and still sharp when taken literally. Being told you'll be hanged does indeed concentrate a man's mind wonderfully. If not always in the right direction. The old gentleman's meaning was that the man should turn his mind towards God. Nowadays he'd be thinking of selling his story to the press.

Mr Charles' mind registered a road sign, a change of direction saying 'Le Havre'. A haven, a harbour – was that what he needed? Maybe he was being followed still? He didn't know and by now scarcely cared. Something in the background of his mind, and he was crossing the Seine estuary before – this was the Pont de Normandie. Very beautiful it was too. After building it the French were overcome by admiration for their own genius, and ran the journalistic phrases for having one's breath taken away deep-deep into the ground. Never mind, astounding will do. It is tall, slim and white; it is aerial, graceful, weightless. It fleets across the estuary (on the sunniest of days a most depressing sight) in a truly Homeric fashion. Straight out of the Iliad: Ajax picked up his enormous boulder; Achilles began to run, shaking the earth. Apollo, blinding in the sunlight, broke the celestial long-jump record.

Now Athene – he was trundling through the industrial glooms of the harbour's outskirts – interpose your shield, and blind the pursuers. He had just remembered where it was that he wanted to go.

An odd lump of land between the Seine and the Somme estuaries; an obscure and as it were forgotten corner of Normandy. Dieppe and Fécamp have at least harbours; so do Harfleur and Barfleur, or did when Henry the Fifth landed there and made himself for a brief moment of intoxication King of Paris too. But Etretat has nothing at all but a shallow shingly bay and a chalk cliff worn into needles. What on earth can be special about it? Something about the light: Manet went there, and Courbet and, er, Delacroix. Boudin! – flocks and flocks of painters both French and English, and John who had never been was curious to understand why.

Normandy coastal village, and a typically dolls' house affair. As was usual, in two halves; the inland village with featureless administrative buildings barracked around a dusty square full of parked cars, and a kilometre further the old fishing village cramped into a little bay between two massive headlands. Two or three streets of small houses in the local stripy style of timbering and plaster; much like what the English call Tudor, perhaps a bit narrower, crookeder, probably darker and dirtier. Fish and chips, bogus pewter and painted pottery, and a great deal of ye-olde lettering. Reminded him of the treasure maps he had made occasionally to amuse the children on wet afternoons: the coloured felt-tip pens, the conventional pictographs for hill and estuary, marsh and sand-dune, and plenty of information in squiggly gothick writing. Seaward adding a caravel or two, and a compass rose. One held it in the smoke of a candle to age it properly, letting the flame char it at the edges . . . the children got bored even before he did, but by then it was nearly supper time.

The holiday season was long by; a few depressed tourists straggled languidly along the front, or climbed the worn paths to the chalk cliffs. Up there a few Verdurins would have country houses, just as they did on the other, Proustian side of the Seine estuary; windswept, but fine views.

There was nothing here for him, but he had run his head into a pocket, was extremely tired, and perhaps he had shaken off – if only for a few hours – the Kindly Ones who were pursuing him. Above all, it was a still, and warmly sunny autumn evening. He would stay the night and hope to get his head clear. He found a hotel room with a balcony, immediately above the front and the dismal pebble beach. The sun would set in the sea, right in front of him. And perhaps there would be a green flash. He installed himself with an armchair and a beer, to think. No thought came. The sun set, prettily enough in an obvious way. No cloud to make it interesting. A nice mauve afterlight over the Channel. Of course there was no green flash. Had he thought they'd lay one on, specially for him? What had he expected?

He felt chilled; put on a jacket, walked out in search of somewhere pleasant to eat. All the places were the same and so were all the menus. Fish, flesh or herring; sounding and looking as though lying here in wait for him, these last six weeks and worse. His dinner and bottle of wine were those one wishes to forget, as soon as may be.

This was Simenon country. They lived here in creakings of old worm-eaten wood, in smells of dust and stale shrimps, peeping from behind lace curtains that could do with a good wash: the jerry hadn't been emptied that morning, either. A lot of bad apple schnapps. Complaints about taxes and the price of fish. Proust killed rats, thought about horrible lesbian goings-on in the house of Mademoiselle Vinteuil. What the hell were painters thinking of, to come here?

But in the morning a clear mind, a clear head, a clear purpose. A grey drizzle on the sad stones, and one of the worst breakfasts it had ever been his misfortune . . . but now he had made his resolution. He would go home. Inasfar as it is a 'home' – no, no, let's have no further messing, no further aimless dodging around . . . straight home. Confront whatever happens. With serenity; it is time

41

to be a man. Stop to rest, yes, for a meal, yes. Take time but do not hang about, in Rouen or Paris or anywhere else. Go home, settle your affairs, live as though you would live forever, and live ready to die tomorrow. There are souvenirs, there are regrets. What point or purpose have either?

PART TWO

*A Chapter
of Accidents*

He should phone the Peartrees. Tell them he was coming; he didn't. Perhaps they were watched; perhaps listened to. That was surely nonsense. He was a tired, old man, driving the Paris autoroute, not enjoying it. Telephones, to Mr Charles, were still switchboard girls, telling him there'd be a twenty-minute wait; it always became three-quarters of an hour. He was of the age that wrote letters. In Paris the 'pneumatique', enchanting invention; the hiss and whistle of compressed air, the loud clack of the polished metal shell – in large shops still, in his childhood.

The written word; an art to postcards, to telegrams, of compressing phrases, without ambiguity.

At school one had learned this; the making of a précis, the condensing of some windbag's two pages into a single paragraph. The arts of memo, the marginal minute, the celebrated half-sheet of notepaper. He had been told off, for rambling, for loquacity. 'Charles, you are a garrulous child.' Launched upon the career of writing, learning to correct page-proofs without expensive over-running.

Books today were not like this. The longer the better: people pick up a microphone and the computer pours out a flood of mumble. Somebody phones you from Dayton, Ohio; half an hour of coughing and a speech with no subject, no verb, and no object. What was it all about? They wanted it faxed by tomorrow morning and it mustn't be over three hundred words, but it took them all that time to say so.

Mr Charles would prefer to put it on a postcard but it would take ten days to arrive if he did, and nobody would understand it.

The Peartrees are not a bit like this. They are frugal with words, because words on the phone cost money. Were the sky to fall, earthquake or invasion of the Saracens, they would mention it in the most guarded as well as briefest manner. An ingrained conviction that 'the government' is listening to every word you say, and writing it all down. 'Our phones are tapped.' The hundred-year-old French legend of 'the dossier'. They might not be all that far wrong, at that.

He does generally phone, out of politeness, after an absence of weeks or months. To tell them 'Back tomorrow', meaning air the rooms, stock the fridge with milk and a sausage, drop me off a loaf of bread. They are laconic. 'Yes. To be sure. Shall do.' And finish with a politely French and flowery enquiry after his health and well-being.

It isn't necessary. He has only been away a few days. The central-heating has been left on trickle. He will get in late, after a pub meal, will want only to go to bed and think about shopping in the morning. (Mr Charles has made himself into a competent, even accomplished cook.)

Perhaps he disregarded a warning. On the Paris road, outside Mantes-la-Jolie, that archetype of French hellhole, it had rained, the road was wetly glistening. On the autoroute – at speed – access roads come in both right and left. There are many peremptory road signs writ large. Versailles, Marly-le-Roi, what a lot of former-royal-hunting-lodges in the forest.

Some silly bugger (no no, pardonably panicked) had come shooting in, mistaken the Paris-straight-on for some suburban destination, changed lanes a bloody-sight-over-abruptly, skidded, overturned; there he was in the middle of the road upside-down and being hiked out of it by the fire-brigade. There are people in orange jackets, and a gendarmerie minibus full of the Emblems of Mortality. These, like the uniforms of their attendant slaves, are of orange plastic. It is an ugly way to die. Trivial, and there is no dignity about it.

The road is cool. Impersonal, unemotional. It does not say, this is the way to the sorrowful city. Here we do not indulge in literature. We do not quote from Dante, nor even from a more modern poet. 'In this house, Monsieur, one does not chat. One counts.' We have made you this road. It is as broad, as smooth, as the best of modern engi-neering can encompass. We have put up large, very expensive, extremely beautiful blue and white notices everywhere, telling you everything you need to know. We have added, in our goodness, everything the heart could desire; petrol, food, police, and games for the children. There are also lavatories, whores and telephones. In some of our choicer rest areas you can even have your stressed nerves and fatigued muscles massaged into calm and con-tent. If you insist upon killing yourself (which will cause inconvenience to others) we are nowise to he held liable.

Mr Charles swung round Paris. What a sonorous and poetical set of syllables is 'Boulevard Périphérique'. Continued Dijonwards, and without slowing down.

Stopped, in a plastic tent, orange, full of plastic palm-trees, for something to eat. For the car to eat, which is even dearer.

To be sure, if you could bear to tear yourself away from this path there would be roadside inns, Relais de Diligence, where Dickensianly one would drink a glass of cherry brandy while the horses were being changed. Menus gastronomiques and touristiques. And there might also be a good-pull-up for lorry drivers, where one would eat better. But you don't really think seriously of quitting the autoroute, because you have paid a hell of a lot of money to be allowed on it in the first place.

And whatever one did, it came out a horrible meal.

On would have to be very careful. It was a day for the petty disasters, for spectacles forgotten on a restaurant table, for – worse – a credit card left lying in a petrol station (while concentrating on not forgetting one's glasses). Mister Charles is apt, if one could call it that, to fits of almost an epileptic nature, of intolerable clumsiness and absence of mind.

He had been lunching one day with an editor; an urbane man always beautifully dressed; exquisite shirt-cuffs. One had somehow managed to overset a large and beautiful glass of extremely good Bordeaux.

"Have you read *Guy Mannering*?" A man addicted to Sir Walter Scott, as well as having excellent manners.

"Not for some years."

"When you next come to it – Dominie Sampson revives a young lady from a fainting fit with the nearest water, which is in a boiling tea-urn, after first emptying his cup into the sugarbowl."

"I do get the point."

He is a large, shambling fellow, Charles. Long ungainly arms, bony red hands, enormous feet.

One would do well to get home without a mishap. So he did, but when he got home there wasn't any. The house had as they say burned to the ground. A cliché perhaps; there was some smoke-blackened stone wall. But these old houses are full of wood, making for a merry blaze. Naturally the village has a volunteer fire-brigade, cheerful healthy young men who sometimes hold exercises on a Sunday morning. He is good friends with them all, contributes to their fundraising, the fanfare and the yearly 'Bal des Pompiers'. It is difficult to imagine them actually putting out a fire. They'd have to get out of bed, for a start.

As with most shocks one doesn't feel it at first. One says like Sister Heavenly, 'Well now, isn't that just lovely!'

There is of course Poirier, upset and apologetic.

"I didn't know where you were. No means of getting in touch. The gendarmerie say it's criminal, all right. The lieutenant was here this morning. Asks for you to get in touch. I was woken by the dogs. Came as quick as I could. Nothing I could do. Went up like a match. So I thought, what can I think of. So I phoned Monsieur Alain." And there is Alan, who has had a long drive, and is completely unflapped.

"Hello, Pa." Alan is the younger of his sons, early thirties, as tall and broad as himself, a great deal quicker on the feet. In mind too, one dares say. Himself has what the French call 'esprit d'escalier'; one thinks of witty things to say on the way downstairs. Hence, possibly, the habit of writing things on pieces of paper; they sound better after a bit of polishing.

Alan's jokes are spontaneous. He does not congratulate himself as openly as his namesake, but like Alan Breck Stewart, 'Am I not a bonny fighter?' fits him well enough. And now mercifully, he finds everything funny.

"Well now, now you're on your bare arse, huh? Know the feeling. Good that you're here, have you an insurance man? Better give him a call, that is if you can remember his name. I can stay a day. If you want me. Let's go down to the pub, book rooms, have something to eat, I have a disquieting thirst, dare say you have too. Got your passport? Save some trouble with consulates. What d'you lose, really? Knowing you, knit it all up within six months. Plenty of money, haven't you?"

"Oh yes, money's no problem. And the insurance will cover this. There's rather an odd aspect though, which I must tell you."

Gaps, yes, I should damn well think there would be gaps; in whatever it is. A narrative perhaps, if ever I construct something of the sort from the notes I made – and still keep making. Gaps in my mind; right here in my head. Big wide empty boulevard here bang in the middle, on the way from my cortex to the medulla oblongata or whatever. Like this moment, driving down the hill behind Alan: I knew who I was, but whose car is that, and why am I following it?

"Want a beer? Pastis or whatever?" Place has been done up. Alcoves. New curtains and carpets, lots of upholstery. I picked up a menu. Making faces at it no doubt because Alan started to get the giggles. "'Oh you won't get chicken pie, In the El Paso jail.' Or was it Rabbit pie?" The food here is pretty bad; pedestrian is putting it kindly. Rabbit pie is a speciality of la mère Poirier's. A strong- and indeed heavy-handed woman, but light, light fingers for her pastry. "You were going to tell me about that odd aspect."

"Somebody's been shooting at me."

"Ah, now I begin to see what Peartree kept gassing about."

"Well, first you have this business of are they trying to hit

49

you, or maybe just intimidate you, or even simply trying to be funny. So you move off a bit to see what happens. Can't make it out, chap gets shot, poor bugger looks a bit like me. What's the matter with this fellow, he's the short-sighted Mister Magoo, he's highly incompetent or he's just pretending to be and if so why, great number of whys, I'm looking for your views. Now burning my house. I'm not finding this in the least funny." Which wouldn't for an instant stop Alan behaving as though it were all uproarious. But he's not going to allow his father any little whiff of self-pity, or any shadow of an attitude: the old man is a figure of farce. Shooting him will have its funny side but blowing him up in some ludicrously complicated catastrophe will be better still.

He has been reading, some Sunday paper, of depredations caused by the sticky-fingers crew. Thieves drive a truck in, these days, clear the entire field, so that farmers, gardeners, growers or whatever you like are now at high risk; Alan relishing the more imaginative countermeasures.

"Geese, sure, ancient Rome, no? – isn't that in Livy, already? What do they do when they raise their voices? Hiss, isn't it? Do they clatter with their wings or is that storks?

"Now pigs are good, especially as I learn when crossed with wild pigs; the more alert, you see, and the more ferocious. Point one of those with tusks up the bugger's arse, oh yes, definitely. From the angle though of raising the alarm, your pig would have to wear a wire perhaps, hook him up to the amplifying system, no?"

"Hark hark, the pigs do bark;

The Beggars are coming to town."

Alan has a strange laugh, silent, interior; it used considerably to irritate Sibylle.

"Bit late in the day, to be thinking of protecting you.

Can you think of anyone who'd like to kill you? Rather a rhetorical question; depriving you of speech would be something else altogether." Make no mistake. With his son Alan he has a better relationship, one needing less speaking, than with anybody. With his elder son, Jaimie (known to Alan as Shem the Penman) he gets on admirably well, make no mistake about that, either. With his daughter, Cathy, special too and highly so; she's the daughter, and the only one. But with either, no point in denying it, a great deal of talk. Here, Alan and he, eating their dinner (nothing marvellous but nor is it in the least a bad meal and in perfectly comfortable pleasant surroundings), taking their time, couple of bottles of wine, stretch out and relax, they neither have nor need a great deal to say.

"Were they any books; couldn't be replaced, that is?"

"Publishers have file copies; apart from whatever the mice haven't eaten in the Library of Congress or the Bodleian."

"Oh, I didn't mean yours." Much contempt. "Anything of value."

"Books do furnish a room." The writers one both loves and respects – they aren't going to create a stampede. The books one wanted to keep had come off sixpenny stalls, in the days when there were such things. Had never been exquisitely rebound. Most professionals one might guess would share the 'Bagshawe' stand-point. One has a lot of books. Rubbish, mostly.

"Pictures?" There now, there had been a few pictures. He cheered up to think that one had got rid of most. One keeps them awhile, to see if they are any good – how the paint sinks in to the canvas. A couple, there were, one was extremely sorry . . .

"There was that portrait, of your mother."

"Oh God, yes." But he cheered up more, to think that

the bronzes had all gone ten years ago. Even fiddled blind by the dealers in Köln he had got good prices. Mark, for good stuff; there had been a young girl, by Georg Kolbe, yes and a Picasso too, an 'Old Man's Head' of 1906. He had given a ridiculous price for that, in New York as a young man. Luckily a very good one (and the right size, eleven centimetres, perfect) so that over the years one had come out ahead. FAR ahead and it more than made up for the boring Henry Moore which had lost its value. Would a bronze have resisted the fire? The insurance premiums had decided him. Must have a grin upon his face; Alan was regarding him with amusement.

"Not a damned thing, I'd say. Isn't that very lucky, and at my age."

"Am I following? – you mean that when young one can replace it all but when old there's nothing one really has to replace?"

"I suppose so, roughly, but Alan – who wants to kill me? Who'd want to burn my house down? Who wishes to hurt me?"

"Is it certain that there's no coincidence? The police say they've no good conclusive pointer. One never will, I dare say – but be grateful perhaps. Pity about the Peartrees, but weren't you rather too comfortable, rather too well dug in? I shouldn't have said you were finished, as an artist. But isn't this something to be glad of? Get a little flat, maybe in London, very small and simple."

"Negation of all principle."

"Oh, you still have principles. At your age, what a horrible surprise. Let's have some coffee, shall we?"

One hadn't needed to run out to buy a toothbrush. There are clothes of which one will always say that it's impossible to find anything that comfortable now. Or the preposterous collection of silk dressing-gowns that from a mania when the children were small had petrified into a tradition lasting ten or twelve years. His suitcase in the car held temperate European clothes and he wasn't about to set sail for the tropics; nor the Arctic.

The books drift into every room, inexorably; the tides lap round them. Now and again one thinks of a purge; one will not endure this squalor. Yet every book, however bad, has devotion in it; love and faith, sweat and torment. Who am I to throw it away? This encrustation of yellowed paper, rotting gently down with the passing moons, is myself. I can say that it is worthless, that I do not miss it. In vain.

In the car I found a forgotten paperback. Like a tatty package of Kleenex, sordid as screwed-up sandwich wrappings, brought along for lonely restaurant tables, solitary hotel rooms. Blessed, now, for being the sole-survivor. It is also a good book, well-written by a good man.

Venture into the Interior, and through this sour smell of burning I embark on a journey into my own withinness.

Journalists have invented the cutting phrase, the 'Kleenex writer' to be read and thrown away, leaving no trace. Just so have I picked to pass an hour from the tidewrack, content for it to be as though 'never before seen'. Mister Charles is not this sort of writer, has an honest pride in the knowledge that work of his has been kept, honoured, reread. In the long years since Sibylle left him, there was little other reason for survival.

A good house this had been, for the writer, full of quiet, a heaven after rackety voyaging; the fruit, too, of the romantic imagining, the vulnerable longings of childhood. Since Sibylle left, an empty, worthless shell.

Here in the hills are sudden violent storms. Lightning knocks out a transformer station. Electricity here was rambling and antiquated, far removed from the nuclear power they boast of, often indeed an improbable patchwork, local peculations straitening regional parsimony, and all dating from the years between the wars. One was reminded that this is a Latin country: we often waited for twenty-four hours before the thing flickered and restarted. The modern toys, mixer or razor or calculator (we opened cans of ground coffee with the tools of the twenties), could be set aside without pain. A fire of birch logs reminded us that for a hundred years this house had existed comfortably without central heating. We rested our eyes, and reposed our spirits, we remembered the region's painters – like Georges de la Tour – lit kerosene lanterns (Aladdin lamps are a focal point of John's English childhood, and Jewishly seven-branched candlesticks of Sibylle's; under English bombs, no German could complain of Semitic Sabbat-eves). We forget, now, the power and the meaning of Light.

So, too, Colonel van der Post, upon an African mountain, fifty years ago. Mlanje, an extraordinary mountain, populated by extraordinary trees; nowhere else found . . . he thinks, and writes, about light, and living among trees; about the young forester who lives on this mountain, alone with his wife and a small baby, in innocence and in happiness because the trees are not like human beings; they are not abject; they are sinister, but not evil: and who will be killed, in the stupidest of accidents, under the writer's eye. A prolonged, a profound meditation upon the nature of good and evil, and upon the rift – deep, uncrossable – within the human being.

Looking at the burned blackened walls John felt relief from a burden; something akin to joy. He was free of this house. Without Sibylle it was nothing, it was a trap, he was well rid of it. Alan, he suspected, had known this, instinctively, already.

The Colonel, and I take off my hat to him because he was

a quarter century ahead of his time, found in the land-
scapes of Africa (the word must include everything that is
marvellous; the peoples, the wonderful animals, the skies by
day and by night) a quickening in himself, an alertness and
sensitivity most impressive to a reader fifty years later. To be
sure, he sees an African now barely imaginable, almost
intact (the planes of 1950 took three days to get from Cairo
to the Cape). He has fought, the Colonel, through the war
in the far east; he has been a prisoner of the Japanese; he
has seen terrible things. Now he is quickened further still,
for this Africa is not as far distant as he had thought from
the pristine and magical Africa of his childhood.

His prose too quickens, becomes lyrical, in a way to
make one smile for he is a fairly pedestrian writer, but his
thinking is good; the more impressive since the Colonel is
still both highly military and extremely British in his viewpoints: he is filled for instance with an awestruck, stunned
respect for the gentlemen of the colonial administration,
all still behaving as though sanctified by the shadow of the
great white queen, and every one still the sweet, just,
boyish master.

I'm awestruck too; one hadn't expected him to have
long-range, condor's eyes able to see far across and over
mountain ranges. He sees murder about and everywhere
present, in our hearts and in our deepest selves. The murderer is powerful and respectable. He has a clean morning
face, is well-spoken, good manners and fine clothes.
He sits with the judges, and our laws are for him.

When I first read this book, which must have been
towards 1960 and close to the beginnings of my own early
efforts as a writer, I was struck by what then seemed a
minor point. The murder is within us, and 'vicarious
adventures in the footsteps of Holmes, Wimsey and Poirot'
cannot lessen the awareness. He is making the point that

murder, tidied up and titivated, could be trivialised. 'Real' murders were written up in the *News of the World*, in the language thought suitable for the servants; 'intimacy then took place'. For the 'educated' class there weren't enough real ones and those sordid: altogether too much squalor even when passion had been bowdlerised into boredom. But fiction supplied the demand. You could have two or three new ones a week; earnest and humourless with clues like a crossword, and guess-the-villain before the obligatory disclosure on the last page, or giggly and fluffy with little sudden shrieks amidst the endless tittering.

Publishers loved this stuff; the market for it was insatiable; it could masquerade as naturalism, even realism; even as art. Some pretty good writers got caught up in this, and some pretty bad ones did very well. Write about a crime, preferably a murder, and it took much brassy self-advertisement as well as plenty of talent to escape triviality. I ought to know something myself of the musical-chairs game, and of finding oneself sitting between two of them. I have now of course for many years enjoyed the pleasant existence of the minor man-of-letters; never rich, and never obliged to chew up and swallow smelly old bits of alligator either. I should hope that I never got too pleased with myself.

I should think now that I have equally an obligation not to be sorry for myself. Salutary to be given a jolt, the more when one doesn't know where the jolt comes from, nor why.

The much bigger jolt, of seeing a man I don't know from Adam, whose misfortune was to resemble me vaguely in appearance and to cross my path at just the wrong moment, knocked over, badly injured – will he recover? How long will it take? May he be even obliged to carry a handicap, for all his days? I fell into a panic, I ran away, my behaviour was abject.

But now; this is interesting too. Abruptly, a large area of my certainties and comforts have been kicked out here from underneath my feet. Another game of musical chairs? – bump, I find myself sitting on a hard, cold, and draughty floor and without the accustomed cushions under my bottom – who the hell is playing a game with me? One thinks of the phrase that made Hardy famous, about the President of the Immortals finishing his sport with Tess. There are several good jokes concealed here. Who says that burning my house down has anything to do with Hardy (better at poetry than at prose to my thinking) being a Grand Literary Figure rather than a scribbler of murder stories? A lot of books burn. A foxy old paperback survives (I had taken it to read in bed with some vague notion of Africa seen with a strong, vivid eye, an eye accustomed to the distances being all wrong in this clear mountain air, to looking over the sights of a rifle . . .) And finding myself being told off, by the Colonel, for writing trivial little murder stories masquerading as art.

Oh yes, I have a lot to think about. Grateful for having here a comfortable room, a warm bed, plenty to drink, Alan's company.

So that he got up and went downstairs undaunted by the dingy mustiness of a French provincial ostlery at breakfast time, by the dispirited somnolence with which the breakfast is brought; by the nastiness of this which is passing as suitable and pleasant at the breaking of a fast. What will be the point of saying a word? People are permeated by the certainty of their own excellence. They may listen, more or less politely, but they'll never do anything about it. No iconoclasm can shake the impacted clichés of the 'full English breakfast' or 'les croissants bien chauds'.

"I say, you're in rather good form." Alan, refreshed by overhearing the thought spoken.,

"True, true. Resolutions were taken. Not just to sit. Sit up, perhaps, crack the whip a little, look around and take an interest instead of falling into a light doze."

"As though his only plot
To plant the bergamot."

"Precisely. And then this whatever it is, that's pursuing me – is it a meteor? Corbleu, let us confront the meteor."

"A great improvement on seeing you palely loitering, I was getting quite worried."

"Yes, well, might not last."

"Nothing does. I can go home, tell Lettice, she was worrying." Letizia is Venetian; a.k.a. Tiziana. Alan may well be very proud of her; we all are. Yes, she is pretty and she's this and she's that and all of it at high power, and funnily, Sibylle who came out of the Ruhrgebiet looked a lot more Titianesque with her lovely curvy nose, a great deal more Venetian.

"One thing, Alan, that embarasses me. I've got this huge great pistol in the car, exactly like the French."

"Good God, can't leave it there."

"Right, I was creeping about being intimidated, in fact much worse, trembling you know and terrified and telling myself that this would make me Feel Braver and now knowing the thing's there makes one feel a perfect fool, perhaps you wouldn't mind taking it."

"What would I do with a thing like that – throw it over the bridge."

"Risky, that; pity, too."

"Give it to the gendarmerie. I take it they don't know you have it? Tell them you found it in the garden, anything a bit mysterious, capture the imagination, stimulate their zeal a bit."

"Alan, this is perhaps an idea. Pity though, rather a good one, they'll freeze on to it."

"Better than being frozen on to it yourself."

"There's that. I'll be living out of the car too, in the foreseeable future. Look, you'll give my best love to Lettice, not going to come and Squat on her, she'll be relieved. And will you ring Cathy for me?"

"Spanish newspapers full of the hot news, you think? Famous writer's house burns down, the Ayatollah strikes again? Boy, you Old, you but definitely not Newsworthy."

"No, but she might try to ring me feeling kind, that it's my birthday or something."

"All right; I like myself to have a chat with ol' Cath." He will talk about his sister. Of whom he is fond; good that his father should be reminded. Alan does not mention his mother. Of whom he is not just fond. But he was always like this. Kindly, gentle, patient, and very, very tactful. Oneself, one doesn't even know where Sibylle is to be found. He does, though.

"Where are you heading for, any firm ideas?"

"No, I don't know. Somewhere frivolous for a start. This is still an address, right? In *Who's Who* or wherever. I'll have Poirier hold any mail. I'll give an instruction to the bank. I'll have business held in London or New York by the agency. I'll give you a ring from Helsinki or somewhere. Lettice, let me hold you. Say nothing, let me cuddle between your bare breasts."

"Costs a magnum of Krug, that," said Alan. "Man – taking Lettice's top off – that's the Pont de Normandie."

John laughs, thought Alan. (One would like some more coffee. Not in this dump, though.) Feeling a strong inclination towards a quiet day, even a lazy day; Letty would quite certainly not be expecting one before nightfall. It is, yes, a goodish distance to home (Alan lives near Versailles).

Now there is one of the things that the old man has never understood, doing whatever he damned well likes and refusing anything that might risk boring him. Some people will call that unselfconscious but others will call it self-indulgent. I'll drive back in the Porsche and it will be easy. The old man would be grumbling and making heavy weather all the way to Paris. This act of wearing dirty old clothes, driving a dirty old car, saying you don't give a damn for anyone – isn't that just as bogus as appearing in a Ferrari when you should be in a Volkswagen. Other side of the same penny is how that strikes me. Getting very miserly too in his old age.

But he laughs, still. Full-hearted, full-throated. Whereas how seriously all the geniuses take themselves. Now this idea of someone wanting, or trying, or maybe just threatening to assassinate him. Paranoid fantasies of elderly writers, what! House burned down? Good thing too, give old dad a jolt. Incidentally, there were some good things in the garden. Besides a talk with Peartree, be an idea to have a word with a local nurseryman.

That Ol'Dad should start enjoying himself again . . . never been good at enjoying himself; always preferred being miserable, really. Had a lousy childhood, of course. And Sibylle – we love her dearly but what a Calvinist.

One day in Alan's house (a suitable venue, it had been felt) the old man had been interviewed; bright young woman from some Sunday supplement. He'd been quite funny.

'Now, Mr Charles . . .'

'Not Mr Charles. Real name is John Charles McQuaid.'

Letty pokerfaced, plying everyone with drinks. The young woman unwisely seeing an imaginary opening, starting in on his childhood, finding him unresponsive.

'Yerss. Yerss.' Sounding just like Ingmar Bergman:

indeed Alan did (and Cathy would) recognise what they called his magic-lantern voice, often a sign of something that unexpectedly moved or upset him.

"'Tom fell out and hurt his knee
And then there was no one left but me.'"

"Oh. Stevenson, isn't it?"

"It is," in a deep doom-laden voice. "The Child's Garden. Would one rather the false commercial jollity, the coy intolerable tweeness of Winnie the Pooh?"

Because he'd seen at once his mistake. The desolation of his childhood was not going to be discussed with the Sunday Thingummy.

You've lots of money, you tight-fisted old bugger. Move it about a bit, enjoy yourself. Living out of suitcases awhile won't hurt you, quite the contrary. There's plenty left in you (Alan's view; Cathy agrees). Got all shut in and dried out. Needs sun and air, wind and rain, a bit of scenery to fertilise.

For who of us (wondered Alan) couldn't find ghastly childhood experiences to put forward in mitigation of enormities, explanation of eccentricities? Who has eaten their porridge in bland and blameless equilibrium? Being yelled at or whacked – indifference is surely far more damaging, but isn't this the most banal of truisms? Really, Alan – he'd say – I had no idea I'd brought you all up so well. Oh well – fire and ice, anyhow preferable to a bath of lukewarm toffee.

PART THREE

A Winter Journey

An-on-ym-ity. Or as far as I know, as far as I can see. No one appears to have followed me, no one takes the faintest interest that one could tell; I am pleased even if it could disconcert me and perhaps it does. The name Charles is colourless, recalls no musician or footballer popular with the young, and it is useful that I have made no television appearances in recent years; nobody is going to look across a room, do a double take, whisper to a companion. Great advantages there are to being old and a back number.

This of course is a capital city. There's never been anything provincial about Amsterdam; only tourists look out for celebrities or gawk when they're to be seen doing their shopping. Good, I don't want to get shot at, and please, don't anyone else get shot on my account. (I phoned the hospital to ask the news of that man. I had the greatest difficulty in getting a bored secretary to grasp what I was talking about: when at last she did – 'Oh yes, him, uh, they did some surgery and that went quite well, I believe, because they airlifted him back to England to a hospital there, I don't know the name of the town but I suppose I could look it up for you if it's important.' She's no worse than any of us. They'd be interested if they were looking after him still. Off their hands and there's no further interest at all. I'd be the same. Too much clamours for our attention.)

Prinsengracht, where the canal is broad, up towards the Brouwersgracht. Expensive but not all that; nice little flat, only two rooms but Dutch-style, window top-to-bottom, flooded with light and a balcony too. Maybe I'll make something out of this, I don't know yet. I've always liked this town. No longer as modish as a few years ago, when it became insufferable. The fashionable-intelligence, as Dickens calls it, has moved on to Prague. Poor Prague.

Behind him he left a France of westerly winds and driving rain showers, of dark cloud masses that came rolling up behind one, slow-seeming, unhurried, but however fast the little man went, scuttling in the fast lane, they always caught one up. The newspaper at lunchtime was filled with ghastly tales of huge relentless rainfalls bucketing down upon the eroded plateaux of the south, of kindly picturesque rivers bellowing like maddened bulls, snatching cars and trees and houses and flinging them about.

Very pleasant, to pass the frontier and find that the physical realities of a northern folk, speaking a Germanic language and building in brick, meant a weather change much more startling, of wind-still calms and foggy frosty breaths, of pitch-black waterways with shiny crinkly skins of ice upon them, of shaggy white pine trees like vegetable polar bears, of prim grey and silver fields and black crows flying.

Flattened under this iron-heavy sky Holland was smaller even than usual, a mediaeval landscape of Brueghel or Avercamp, full of hooded dwarfs sinister in shapeless padded jackets.

"Had quite a drive, haven't you," said the woman at the desk, her painted nails picking at the keyboard; indifferent, not looking for an answer. "I've a notion you just got in in time, the forecast is freezing rain and black ice."

Dutchly different and pleasurable (he likes this country, these knuckly obstinate people) the cosy coffee-shop womb, the Scottishly varied breads at breakfast, tender and crunchy, baps and beschuit, you won't find an English word for either – nor French, 'biscottes' so much nastier . . . Sitting on a Dutch lavatory pan, 'wrong way round' with the exit at the front . . . the enormous bony girls . . .

"Koffie?" asked the house-agent's young woman, nodding at the percolator on her desk. "I could have something quite nice for you and it's almost next door." These interiors glowing with heat, grey-painted but with masses of flowers; they've flowers here the way the English have pint milkbottles, the way the French have rude little women.

"Just as well if it is next door." Black ice has coated everything in gleaming treachery. An Amsterdam quayside switches disconcertingly from cobbles to cement paving to sand-bedded bricks at the best of times. Since dawn the busybees have been at work with sand and sawdust – salt is not earth-friendly but girls use it to get that glibber-glatter off the steps, I don't intend to get sued for any broken hips.

"Give you the key to look, shall I? Oh, and the heating's turned off but you'll find the temperature-control just inside the door."

One has known it seal a car totally, so that neither door nor window will open, just as for a publicity photograph a bottle of vodka can be enrobed in a cylinder of ice. It has not occurred to one to try and imagine the view from the inside outward, because there isn't any. He flicked a hallway light to verify the mains, turned the heating switches to their maximum; the smell of stagnant air was to be expected. In the empty living room he wondered whether the Dutch, betimes a hideously clever people, had invented a new sort of venetian blind. almost as though candlewax had gutted down the panels. It took a good moment to realise that the rain, on the outside glazing of the bay . . . so that the feeling of being on the inside of the iceberg – easily one might be struck by a claustrophobia, hammering with a crowbar, hoping to find a weak spot; there, where a little light trickles through – the ice can be no more than a centimetre or two thick.

It was not altogether unpleasant. The silence. Quiet would be the most expensive of luxuries. Country quiet, which he had lost, was a romantic delusion and surely always had been. The cocks had crowed and the dogs had barked. The wheeled cart had been as noisy as the tractor, and the blacksmith's hammer as irritating as a chain saw. War and plague had always threatened; the clank of armed men or the scuttle of rats as sinister as the racket of a scouting helicopter. He had known the flutter of a trapped butterfly against a windowpane to be as maddening as a pneumatic road drill.

Town quiet – oh yes, to be sure; high above the ground, in a seventeenth-century house in the Ile-Saint-Louis, traffic-free; a modernised apartment triple-glazed; a building with polished parquet even on the fourth-floor landing, where occasionally one's path crossed that of academic old ladies in quilted dressing-gowns. 'And how is Madame de Sévigné this fine morning?' A little chat, some hot gossip, the very-latest from 'my son-in-law, who is Chef de Cabinet to the Minister' and then a long lamentation about those damn pigeons again, making messes on the balcony.

Amsterdam – here looking out over the water, upon one

of the oldest, most civilised canals in the city – if one could get those windows opened the racket would be deafening.

He stood looking at the wall of glass, where the guttering trickle had stiffened into a stalactite of three metres' breadth, sealing him in, as though he had fallen into the crevasse of a glacier.

He was on the inside of a candle. Those candles that Sibylle used to buy for the children towards Christmastide, the time of candles. Square, cunningly devised, a softer wax within which burning down illuminated the harder outside crust into a magical semi-tranparency. Some were scored or scratched on the exterior and the flame lit lacy wavering patterns.

Others again had little windows, with scraps of transparent coloured paper stuck on, to imitate stained-glass, gothically lit by the moving flame within.

So that I remembered Proust's magic lantern, lighting Golo riding to the castle, and Geneviève of Brabant.

I am inside the candle. Out there, in the murderous sharp-spiked daylight of an Amsterdam winter, is perhaps my enemy. Across the canal, it might be, with a rifle. He cannot see me. Between us is this mask, a thick-trickling treacle of ice over the glass panels, sealing too the aluminium joins. I cannot open them, I am a prisoner, I cannot walk out there on the balcony, saying, 'Here I am. Go on then. Try.'

What am I doing here, anyhow? This is all wrong, this is not the city for me. I want to feel people close to me, I wish for street sounds and smells, I want to reach out, to touch, and be reassured that I am still alive.

When he thought of it then it was astonishingly easy. Out in the street – give that girl back her keys – John had only to raise his eyes. The sky, this wonderful winter sky, and there above the Leidseplein, floating in it, graceful, as silent as a glider, the big jet, planing down in the spiral towards Schiphol. That, now, would serve his purpose; that is what the thing is for.

This northern land, Rhine land, was wrong. He had wanted to sit in some stuffy, dark café, drinking gin, surrounding by whores? There behind his back, only ten minutes walk, in the harbour quarter – he was going the wrong way. If a winter destination, then Danubian.

It had been much too long a time, since a girl had been in bed with him.

A Danubian journey should be made in autumn? Lazily, leisurely, stopping to see how this year's grapes would turn out, pausing over a series of sun-flushed silky-limbed girls. Past Ulm and past Passau; Linz and Wien and Bratislava.

Not in winter. He had driven all the way up here, wasn't about to turn round and go back again. He would pick up the car and drive, yes, as far as the airport. That is what they are for. Straight through to Budapest.

First, a phone call. To my old mate Kollo. One has lots of acquaintances, but few more suitable to the present state-of-mind.

Kollo is to be sure a disgraceful character. So are most of one's acquaintances. So am I.

"Business or Economy?" asked the ticket girl. "Will it be as cold down there as it is here?"

"Drier," said John, happily. "More snow, less ice." All these kind friends in KLM. They might be a bit late with the take-off. Don't want any black ice forming on our wings. One wouldn't think about this bit – skip straight to the café table, in Budapest.

"Doctor Faustus in the garden, that's me." Kollo had said.

"Doctor Who?" I wasn't used, then, to his style.

"Little fellow there in the corner, applauding,

Aphrodite's getting it on the carpet of buttercups and daisies."

"Priapus perhaps?"

"What I said, no? You're in a lousy business, I'm in a good one, the roxy is the best there is." The first time we'd met and we'd both drunk too much Hungarian champagne.

"Porning become Electra."

"Aphorism, schmaphorism. You are Thanatos, I am Eros. I dance upon the grave of President Codswallop."

His language is inventive, often comic. You can't call us friends but you can say we're friendly, nicht wahr, Herr Cockswallop?

"Like every other business we're drowned in these cheap miserable imitations. Be it soft, tit in a cloud of muslin, or that hard camera looking straight up her hole, it's so boring. First I ever saw, death-in-the-afternoon, I suppose I was fifteen, they're under the shower for three-quarters of an hour, suckyfucky WahWah, died of boredom, said, 'I can do better than that', look, you want another bottle, catch the eye of Rosybottomed Aurora over there? – no? – no. Come over to my place, then I show you."

Budapest is the capital of the industry. This sounds like the opening line of a novel by people I know. Be brisk, move the action about. Chapter Two, 'Sydney is not all bridges and opera houses'. This impression of wind in the hair encourages the pop readership; said to prevent the feeling of wind lower down, which is practically the only joke John Galsworthy ever made. I like a book to be a less breathtaking affair. I want my breath taken, I'll apply to Kollo. One reason for coming here, maybe. Are there any assassins trailing after me? We'll see, and if there are they're running up quite a petrol bill. But Budapest, delightful, is also within the Charles circuit.

There is indeed something special about the girls. Hungarian mistresses were a feature in Hapsburg times and before then, but it isn't only dipping into doxies. Kollo gets passionately technical. 'Cambrure' translates as rather more than 'camber'. I'd suggest 'carriage': how she walks, sits upon a chair or a horse. Her 'ensellure' has a specific reference to her lower back. 'What!' says Dumas' Gorenflot. 'Disturb ourselves to look at other loins than loins of mutton – never!' Kollo's girls don't have loins.

"It's the boys – the boys that are the problem." And earnestly (sounding like Nabokov), "The ugliest, but the very ugliest penis I ever saw." Good taste; yes, I too thought the phrase absurd in the context at first.

"I won't have zoos. I will not use children, and well may you say that you'd hope not indeed, there are plenty who do. What do we make of that?"

"That it's a very dirty world, in any business you care to name, and you are less rank of hypocrisy than – oh, banks."

"The other big problem is humour. Mustn't have any humour in commercial roxy." Alas, and in most movies there's not much room for humour. "Stay away, Fay. Come to the studio in the morning and you can see how it works in practice."

The particular pleasure in the meeting had been Kollo's use of the identical phrase quoted by Marguerite Yourcenar, citing her two maiden aunts who kept the bordel in Ostend; roughly, that there are only two trades really worth practising, 'la bouffe et l'entrejambe'. Food in the stomach, and satisfaction lower down.

It took a little time, next morning, before one began to grasp. Small crew used to working together. Fat cameraman and Kollo in symbiosis. You can get effects to lift your roxy out of the ruck by imaginative use of simple detail rather than by spending a lot of money.

He was looking at a blonde. It wasn't the pleasure it ought to be; one was conscious of curiosity; a tinge of morbidity to that, maybe. Perhaps this was the effect aimed at.

She was thin, seemed young. The bony pallor brought only anaemia to mind: one couldn't call her pretty and to his eyes she wasn't sexy either. She was standing, eyes downcast, greenish. She had straight fair hair, fine and thin, cut an inch below her ears. She wore a crumpled cotton T-shirt and hip-high jeans. What was the point? Kollo and the cameraman muttered together.

She put a hand in her pocket. The side of her trousers dragged a little and suddenly the ensemble was not innocent at all. All that showed was waistband, of white schoolgirl knickers, and abruptly this was vicious, as a showgirl stripping in a bar never ever is. A tension instantly extreme; what would she do next? If her navel is this magnetic . . . John understood that porn is like politics. Shaking hands with everyone is known as 'pressing the flesh'; this is unending but in Kollo's eye there's rather more to it. There are politicians who look imbecile, and are gifted at the work. John is desiring this horrid skinny girl the way Bill wants to be President.

"And he-she-me," said Kollo. "And also Ho Chi Minh."

"Listen, matey, I'm phoning from Amsterdam, I'm bored. I'm also half dead, what have you got that's life-enhancing?"

"I gotta Castle." In a high squeaky voice, much as though Kollo had decided to become a eunuch for the kingdom-of-heaven's sake. "I gotta new car too, to show you. Come on over. Like Brits say, the air here is like wine. Water a bit cold, we'll have Daffodil break the ice with her foot, man, her frostbitten nipples, sensational."

"Did you say Castle?" unbelievingly.

"This time round, we'll make it the nunnery."

"I'm laughing all the way to the plane."

"Revolutionise the roxy is Kollo's motto." In roxy-terms, the convent is nothing very new. A Hungarian Castle is something else.

Big big Cuban cigar in flossy new office with a view of the Danube bridges. Everyone else's industries are on their last legs but not The industry; doing better than ever. John has refused to abandon Cuban cigars, and hopes for a few earthly pleasures-still-remaining.

Now castles; yes, decrepit aristocracy, hard times, family property recovered from post-communist régime, can't afford to keep it up, feeble-minded notions about country-clubs and health institutes, Man, the Roxy Steps In, nobody else got any hard currency. "Terrific garden this one has," putting in the cigar to free his hands for expressive gestures.

"Can't film there in winter surely? – cold, no?" Buda and countryside around were under twenty centimetres of snow; nice powder snow, yes, but still?

"You'd be surprised; you're going to be surprised. The inside is terrific too, the very best kind of castle, eighteenth, maybe seventeenth century Lustschloss on top of mediaeval fortifications, long Gothic passages, sinister cells, a Nunnery scenario, not to speak of dungeons, torture chambers and a moat with waterlilies. The cherry on the surprise is going to be Daffodil."

"That her name, is it?"

"Who knows? Who cares?" One had to leave the reins loose upon his back when in this mood, being expansive. Gilt-edged, the Daff; a new stud too, lovely boy, just out from a stretch in the hokeycokey, learned some manners there too; won't last, little bastard's got the Porsche already. "But this is going to make me the HEAD screwdriver a twelvemonth from now. I'm going to ring up now, say we're on the way."

The new car had a fridge, with champagne in it. And Man – a picnic basket, Fortnum and Mason, the cream, mate, think we were going to Glindyburn or wherever.

"Castle's got a private chapel . . . We'll be doing the nunnery when the weather's warmer. The Daff looks great in those starched white things. Coifs . . . Wimples . . ."

There was a new, Polish cameraman. Mister Charles, I tell you, think we were Ingmar Bergner. Look – sunlight. Marvellous the blue shadows. Virgin snow, Daff's a virgin, can't waste it.

"She'll scream."

"Let her scream. Lay her in the snow, snow's warm, or she's only got to think it is. Teenagers, game of hide and seek in the garden, he'll chase her. It'll be lovely and warm in the caravan and what the hell is she paid for? Lose her cherry in this lovely stuff among the rhododendrons, got to get it right on the first take but that's the spontaneity, see you?"

"Carried away."

"Don't get it all that often ackshally, the carrying away." It was warm in the sun (they were quite high up, here) but in the shade of the heavenly rhododendrons one did get uncarried fast. But funny, yes. 'The children' got crosser while everyone else got weaker from laughing. It's for this he likes Kollo, who yells, cajoles, guffaws. Isn't it the terrible seriousness that makes revolting-roxy?

"Want to see to it that they're enjoying themselves. Can't do any more, or not till it snows again; all trampled. Back to the barn; boring auditions this afternoon. Like Daffodil, do you? Fancy her for the night?"

"Rejuvenating lotion."

"She's a nice girl." Fondly. "She'll do your back. Kind."

"Does she get a little present?"

"No, no, no, one's forever telling her; wipe the corner of

your mouth; been at the After Eights again, be sure she doesn't overeat at breakfast, every ounce on that tumtum costs me." It was like having a stable of boxers; only hungry are they any good.

A nice hotel room. They know me? – they pretend they do, which is just as good, making a fuss of is everything as you like it, Mr Charles? Sloppy, but it's always agreeable to have one's fur stroked the right way, the vanity flattered. I must mention this because a lot of people had pottered in and out; chambermaid with another pillow, and perhaps a thicker quilt if you like to have your window open? Waiter to see whether there was beer in the fridge. It's an old place, full of faded glories; row of bronze bellpushes to summon valets or whatever, none of which work, fairly typical of central european communist régimes. Large rooms and plenty of sitting space, mahogany whatnot to press your trousers, Biedermayer wardrobes whose doors won't shut and whose drawers don't open: I was very comfortable. Quite right not to modernise these bathrooms, though doubtless some idiot shortly will.

Daffodil duly appeared, demure in a long skirt and lugging the travel-bag. Young enough, shy enough to be giggly.

"Ooh, the wonderful bathroom, I love baths, can I have one?"

I hadn't paid any attention to the bedroom side of the room. I was going to take Susie – probably Zsuzsa – to bed, not so much for further dalliance since my capacities are limited but because I am betimes exceedingly physical in reaching out to touch. I was on the sofa with German poetry found in the bookshop that afternoon, next door to earrings for Susie. Insel Verlag, very nice.

'Ich, Bertolt Brecht, bin aus den schwarzen Wäldern.'
And looking forward to

'Als sie ertrunken war und hinunterschwamm
Von den Bächen in die grösseren Flüsse
Schien der Opal des Himmels sehr wundersam' –

"Do you want to wash me?" Daffodil was shouting from
next door.

Yes of course, and I'd rung the floor waiter for a bit of
supper; champagne (Hungarian, French now being in bad
taste) and caviare (red, but with black bread) – the chocolates were his initiative. Really it could have been anyone –
I remember too a handyman who came to change a dud
light bulb. But I am anticipating.

Few delights equal giving a bath to a new mistress; not
that she was, naturally, but there is the soursweet of pretending. And thereafter I put the book down. Daffodil
wrapped in a towelling hotel dressing-gown, fluffy and
slightly moist from steam: she had played lavishly with the
mini-this-and-thats they leave lying around hotel bathrooms; body lotions blah-blah.

"I'll do your insteps shall I? And your back afterwards."
It would have been horrible to suspect Daff. I did, for a
moment (wondering about that bag full of junk as well as
her toothbrush); it was horrible.

But the Interlude (ludic, ludicrous – Se vuol ballare,
Signor Contino?) had also moments of comic relief; somebody out of Kingsley Amis, possibly, muttering about The
Weeping Pleiads Wester to keep in command of states
threatening over-excitement, myself hovering between
Daffodil's mouth and lines by Bertolt Brecht; turning her
over – they are quite right about the Hungarian ensellure. Pretty mousebush too, top and bottom – rich mouse,

fine and soft, really the only 'childish' thing about her.

"Should I shave it?"

"Why not?" in a naughty frame of mind. "Or peroxide it."

No, Kollo would be very cross. Furious this afternoon with a silly girl who's cut hers heartshape, to fit into her swimpants. Shouting, 'What will we do now, cut off bits of mine and glue them on?'

"You have to keep the schoolgirl look. For the nunnery, maybe . . ."

"I can't make out why they make such a fuss. There was this piece in the paper, fifty per cent of Russian teenagers will do it, twenty-five for money and ten with other girls, me it's a hundred all the way if I haven't a stomachache."

"Girls too?" Peculiar that this excites men, d'you think?

"As long as they enjoy. Times they piss and moan, something chronic."

"Do you moan?"

"Like this, Oooooh?"

"No, Like Beu-euh."

"Only in that awful castle which is filthy hot and stinking cold, your back the one and your front the other."

She was – it's sufficiently rare – streets beyond Barbie. Was it abject of me to wish she would change magically into Sibylle? My twenty-year-old and very stiff and virginal Sibylle, whom I filled to the brim with Pernod?

Then there came the moment when I wandered over bedward, looking where the chambermaid had put my pyjamas.

She'd left the little greeting-card on the pillow saying 'Sleep well' – with two chocolates, either side. And right in the centre was a butcher's knife, biggish one, upright, force used, straight down into the mattress. No message; the medium is the . . .

I was not frightened. Suddenly I was damned angry. But

the appalling habit of writers, seeing everything as book material. I thought of Alan. Not mine, but Stevenson's.

This too is very 'writer' – we're a contemptible crew – that in moments of emotion we'll steal the words of our betters, and R.L. was both bad and very good . . . Without understanding a syllable, since her English is cocacola, poor Daff was terrorised. The children to whom I read it aloud knew it as I did by heart.

"Powder and your auld hands are but as the snail to the swallow against the bright steel in the hands of Alan." While picking up the telephone with a shaking hand I gave the naked girl with her enormous frightened eyes the second barrel.

"Before your jottering finger could find the trigger the hilt would dirl on your breastbone." We speak of a 'writer's word' the way a nurseryman will of 'a plantsman's flower' and 'jotter' which contains dodder, totter, judder, is enviable. And pins me to the wall in the one thrust of the dirk.

I had trouble fingering those disgusting little buttons; more getting through. Probably Kollo was in some bordel, if with his mobile-phone glued to the collarbone. Struggle with your goddam collar-button, the girl he had just undressed told Ray Chandler. Detachment was creeping in.

"Listen, Kollo, anybody in your part of the world wanting to be funny and make me shit?"

"Not being hoitytoity is she? I'll have her skull and bones if she starts overacting."

"No no, she's doing my back, she's the Balinese temple girl. But this shop of yours has a peculiar line in pillow talk." I made it as brief as I could; one has trouble being succinct under such circumstances. When Waugh (the father, of course) was a foreign correspondent the paper cabled him for confirmation of a rumour of atrocities. Red

Cross personnel under shellfire; whatever? Rush instant full details.

He cabled back 'Nurse Unupblown'. Few of us manage to be exact and laconic together.

Kollo was for once bereft of speech. A cliché that, but at least it's short. At last he managed "I'll be round inside an hour." It's a pity that 'Round up the usual suspects' should have become another: it is the fate of many good lines.

I was not though going to be like RL's Uncle Ebenezer. I would tremble no longer. We've given that up. It would seem now that you, whoever You are, begin to concentrate on putting me in fear, I shall have to try and find means to broadcast a plain fact. Since you burned my house, I have stopped being frightened. Stimulated, and we'll now put this to the proof. I put both hands on the girl's bare breasts. She shakes and I don't. Her nipples are receptive; I dare say I could find a better word but this is no longer the moment for being literary. For being upright; erect; vain of it. "Strike an attitude, Peaches." Vulgar expression, picked up from Kollo no doubt. He arrived indignant.

"I'll have a heartfelt word with the management here. Grilled the night porter already, place is full of whores but this passes understanding. We admit, our poor people are impoverished, open to bribery, but hotel help, porca madonna, don't want to lose their good job. Don't all work in an honest business like ours . . ."

"Damn, now I've run out of cigarettes."

"Ring the floor waiter, Daff, tell him Gitanes filter and another bottle of champagne, let's start with that bugger." His tail coat was like himself, like the whole place, shiny with wear and a bit greasy. Stevenson's words came back.

'A clappermaclaw kind of look to ye, as if ye had stolen the coat from a potato bogle.' And did it not apply to myself?

*

John, your life needs simplifying.

What, for example, is the point of all this reading and writing? Most of the human race doesn't read: why bother? Decipher a few basic instructions; that's enough.

'Keep these pills out of the reach of children. Do not exceed the stated dose. Respect the instructions of your doctor or pharmacist.'

Which were oral. There's no need to go on reading the small print, a whole paragraph about possible unpleasant side-effects, one of which is reading about them. That is for us, the printed-paper addicts.

One learns as children do, from oral instruction, from example, observation, and Sitting next to Nellie. Most people are technically illiterate. Put them down in the city and the meaning of 'Walk/Don't Walk' will soon appear. The computer says 'Enter'. The ads have pretty pictures, and who speaks of an advertisement? Know Latin'n'everything, do we? The voice-over repeats the winning lotto numbers, slowly, clearly. John knew a successful business man who couldn't read.

"I learned dodges. Shapes; intervals."

"Like road signs? 'Direction Porte d'Ivry'?"

"That's right. Like a Morse Code. And a secretary who reads." He can look at a picture, a building, a landscape. He can hear music. Go to a theatre, a cinema. If he wants it he can get the book on tape, some actor reading it.

These damn notebooks; I've carried them around, virtually since I can remember. Everything I ever wrote took initial shape here. There must be fifty or more, at home. No there aren't; not any longer. American universities won't get them, now. Too bad . . . And since the beginning of this – call it this Adventure – call it what you like, call it 'Kidnapped' (one could make something of this title; wasn't the drift now towards a kidnapping of his life, his personality, his character – a subtle dictation of what he might or should or could do next?) he had put a lot of it between the covers. Lifelong habit, raw material, it might turn into a book. This morning (having nothing else to read) Mr Charles had been turning pages. Taking books away from an addict was, he supposed, very similar to kicking heroin cold-turkey; lock him up and feed him Mars Bars.

Startling, and shocking; on every page, be they scribbles in telegraphese or quite carefully composed passages, were citations, references, paraphrases, from other writers. To be sure, one had always done this. Somebody said, thought, wrote; someone put it neatly, found a good cadence, an original image, a striking coinage. One has relied upon a capacious and retentive memory, now worsening rapidly but at his age, hell, it was to be expected. So that more and more the bits of literature went into the aide-mémoire with the unspoken injunction to look them up when at home and verify.

But this – the addiction had become a grovelling dependence. There was no more home. There must be no more literature. He was in the world now, alone, and could reach out no longer for the comforting hands.

He was reminded now of Roger. Roger is not a writer. Roger is a SDF. It takes so long to say things in French that the wretches put everything in this form; a good language has decayed. Stands for Sans Domicile Fixe; we'd just say homeless, roofless, or on his uppers. According to Roger's Papers, which might be bogus but he doesn't know himself, he is thirty. That would be about right. His face is handsome and intelligent; his physique was pretty good when he was picked up. Badly marked by exposure and malnutrition, but healthy enough. Negative on tuberculosis, AIDS, and alcoholism, which isn't bad for a start. The medical examiner thinks his intelligence is normal. He is well co-ordinated. The police report says 'unaggressive'. Indeed gentle, with an attractive smile. When found he had no possessions but the clothes he stood up in, and a football, in a plastic bag.

Problem; Roger doesn't talk. Roger has only two sentences.

'J'suis tout seul'. 'J'tape dans le ballon'. Mostly he runs the two together. 'I'm all alone and I kick the ball about.'

Who is Roger? The social-assistant did her best with the resources she has. I know her; a gentle and sensitive girl. She's overworked and underpaid; her job is underfunded, undersupported. She has excellent qualifications, is highly experienced. I haven't the time nor energy for a tirade against the City of Paris and nor has she.

She could make little of Roger because he has been obliterated. Misfortune, misery, suffering and want. There's a lot of it about.

Roger knows nothing of himself. Had he a wife, children, parents or relatives? He cannot say. Skills, talents? Beginnings – a birthplace, a home ground? An educational level? He is puzzled. 'J'suis seul, et j'tape dans le ballon.'

We won't, since we needn't, discuss the shortcomings of the City. It has still much beauty, and a unique atmosphere. It's true that every other city looks like a slum in comparison. It is marvellously administered, competent and very clean. It is extremely corrupt; it still makes fewer balls-ups than any comparable city I have ever seen. The poor, on the whole, are pretty well cared for. Were I a clochard – the word comes from 'clocher', to limp or be awry – better to be limpy here than anywhere else. What can they do for Roger?

There's a sickening inevitability to that nothing; thinking

too of the generation to come, the ten- and twelve-year-olds. As hopeless, and far more cynical.

Look at me. All the difference in the world. Privilege, money, the safety net. I will not be picked up by the police. Visible resources, a small talent, which I have done little to merit. Knowing a few people. Losing your house – Alan said it; what importance has it?

There's still more resemblance than I'd care to admit. Since Sibylle left me – J'suis seul, et j'tape dans le ballon. Within my income, of course.

Stevenson's language – the children relished it. 'There's many a lying sneck-draw sits close in kirk, and stands well in the world's eye, and maybe is a far worse man than you misguided shedder of man's blood.' Much can be laid at my door, but not that. Why does the man of blood pursue me?

John has thought of a possible reason; not perhaps as far-fetched as it seems. This lies far in the north, but to fly from Budapest to Stockholm is no more than a variation on getting back to Amsterdam where he has left the Audi, the faithful-truedog. And this might not be what the man-of-blood expects of him. A trail is left, and this time a deliberate trail. If there is an abscess, it must be lanced.

And here he has an ally; an old friend, a good friend. Brigitta is not an ex-mistress. They have slept together, but not so that it would become a comfort-habit. Brigitta does not suck her thumb. Nor did she like thumbsuckers. Had two sides to her head, and liked men who could stand up.

A big girl. She must be well past fifty by now. Big in several senses; quite a massive woman, big Swedish bones and a powerful bosom, lots of fair hair untidy and going grey; broad architectural forehead and wide cheekbones and apple-cheeked; she likes the sun and is always tanned, but not a lie-supine tan: a wind-and-sailingboat tan, and big competent hands and feet. With the promise of more strength, and one isn't wrong to think so.

Stockholm: not a town I know well so I left the car in Hamburg, which I know better, flew in, took buses, took taxis. It is still not late for snowfall and there was plenty; still not late for winter, and the black-and-white city was sombre, still, quietened by the snow-discipline, the car-hysteria slowed and muffled, trying to lessen the pollution by putting brakes on sand and salt as well as speed.

I had phoned, of course. She is a widow, and she's often away. Or there might be friends staying in the flat; there often are. But a tranquil voice answered. At home and much so, and alone, and hey, you're very welcome, and hoy, is it that long a time since we saw one another?

A nice flat in a quiet apartment block and when you look out of these triple-glazed windows you catch glimpses of trees and water. Large, comfortable, untidy, like herself. Book-lined and penetrated by music. She used to be a writer, not a good one but a professional, highly readable, did well and invested wisely, does an agony column in some women's weekly, quite a lot of social and travel journalism, has radio spots and does a bit of television; speaks good German and Danish as well as an effortless expressive English, which is not quite the commonplace people seem to imagine. I'm reaching my point rather slowly: I've much respect as well as liking. I asked her once why she stopped writing fiction. 'Not good enough,' she said, and how many writers who are making money will you hear say that?

Brigitta had on a bluish shift frock, simple.

"You're a sight for sore eyes," we both said together.

"Are we staying in or going out?" she asked.

"Don't want to struggle with all that smoked reindeer today." She threw her head back to laugh; her throat is lined but shapely.

"Meatballs and pea-soup for you then, stinker." I wasn't frightened; she's a good cook, loves to eat and drink and will sink the single-malt with anyone.

"And Bourgogne." Robust in all senses. "Come on in to the kitchen." It's a lovely eclectic living-room full of flowers and some good modern pictures she's had cheap from the painters. The kitchen is scrubbed and Swedish. She produced a goodish bottle, with the promise of a better later, and a big ashtray, and vegetables for me to clean. Olga Havlova – there was a woman to be loved; was her kitchen like this? Smoked Spartas, which are cheap Czech cigarettes while peeling her potatoes, among her friends. Including her man, the Prez. "What's the news then?"

"I am dropping down the ladder rung by rung." She laughed.

So I told her, as simply as I could, what had been happening to me. She took it calm, coolly. Typically she made the point at once, which I have seen, but I've been circling round it, like an incompetent bomb-aimer.

"But this is your Winterreise. Your winter journey through yourself, of exploration and discovery. That it has a crime theme, rather fine that."

"Nice of you to think so." She paid no attention to that.

"Egoism and egotism, twined together, the one reasonable and the other base, ignoble; that's for you to sort out."

"Yes, well, it has its comic side. But suppose they follow me here, and someone flings a bomb and hits Brigitta, that won't be quite so funny."

"Is it pretentious," wiping her knife on her apron, "to suggest that you'll have to accept it? I'd have to, too. Lord, let me not be certified, how long I have to live. An auto might skid and mount the pavement. Some clown turns on the gas, kill their silly self. Neighbour smells it, doesn't think, press the doorbell to say Hey, spark makes a lovely big Pop, building comes down. On me, silly bitch."

"I don't think they'll have bombs – whoever they are. The pattern's very odd but to me it doesn't seem indiscriminate."

She left her meatballs to simmer, took my cut-and-washed cabbage and put it on, sat down and poured herself another glass of the comforting red Hautes-Côtes juice.

"Has it occurred to you that if something happens here you'd have our lovely Swedish Policía to deal with – wouldn't that be fun!"

I ought to explain. We both belong to a past generation, and although Brigitta is a lot younger than myself she knows it too. She was part of the gang, in their youth stuffed with idealism and Communist inclinations. She was at school with the girls (a splendid group of talented and beautiful actresses, I never did sort out which was Harriet and which was Bibi) made famous by Bergman. The conservative, not to say reactionary segment of Swedish society, including all of the police authority, spent much time and effort on (often muscular) discouragement of left-wing sentiment. Cast your mind back – if you are old enough – to the Vietnam years. Brigitta, it's her own words and a fact which amuses her, has a police dossier as long as a roll of shithouse paper.

This period in Sweden culminated, if that's the word, in the assassination of Olaf Palme. Remember? Not all that long ago; it was 1985. And it was never cleared up. Right? Palme was a sympathetic figure, right? That immense rarity among politicians, the man who appears honest, kindly, intelligent, and who expresses the intention to do something about society. He was also rapidly acquiring repute as a statesman of international class. You could say that's a virtually non-existent commodity. Look at the American Presidents since Truman and the word abject becomes insignificant. Look at oh, anywhere. One comes up with Richard von Weiszäcker whose job was honorary and powers limited to speaking. Sweden is a small, inbred, incestuous and exceptionally provincial society, save in its own estimation. Small wonder that there were a great many people anxious to get rid of Palme and no time lost: a great great number of them in Sweden.

Getting interested? I had, too: this was the moment that brought Brigitta and me together.

"We need to think about this," handing me the second bottle to open since I was butler – By God: it was a La Tache. "It's not clear to me at all, these weird attacks. But the principle seems to me to frighten you off, am I right? Frighten you off what? You come here, which seems to me unduly brazen, pretending to be naïve. Boy, if anything should happen to give the Policía an excuse for interference, you could be in deep shit."

Damned Brigitta; it was with real relish that she said it.

The facts aren't in doubt. Or what is known of them isn't. There's far too much one doesn't know and isn't likely to find out, which is why I had gone no further at the time. Experience has taught one that when a criminal enquiry begins to throw a shadow across a government administration, familiar clichés appear and make themselves known. Noses meet brick walls. Clams clam up. Minds are a perfect blank; good memories have these unaccountable lapses. Reports gather dust in drawers whose keys have been mislaid and Mr Thing who was in conference all last week is on sick leave.

Where suspicions lie, including imputations of malfeasance and guilty knowledge as well as sloth and incompetence, we may rely upon any police authority in the world to ensure that the facts stay unknown or unprovable.

Brigitta knows the facts as well as I do. It is exactly ten years ago. Sveavägen, a main street in the city of Stockholm; twenty past eleven on the evening of Friday, February 28th; here on the pavement on the corner of Tunnelgatan, in front of the shop called 'Dekorima'. Olaf Palme, First Minister of the government of Sweden, died here shot in the back. There is now a bronze plaque let in to the pavement here, to remind people. Flowers get left on this. If I need to remind myself, a Swedish woman is here to remind me. It is a safe bet that the police haven't forgotten, either.

Journalists collected many small details, which the police hadn't. Thus, we all know that the murderer ran up the eighty-nine steps, in four flights, leading to Malmskill- – thank you, the name hadn't stuck in my head – -nadsgatan. What had stuck? That the assassin was seen. He had 'Scandinavian looks', while the police were gassing on about wicked Croats, naughty Kurds, and the KGB. That no effort was made to cordon off the inner city. That the alarm was given at only two in the morning, and that the Commissaire commanding the criminal brigade heard about it on the radio over his breakfast. Stockholm's Prefect of Police, a bureaucrat with no experience of a criminal enquiry, would direct all the operations, in an atmosphere of cock-up masking intrigue, the irregular shading into the illegal, rarely seen even in France. We would hear a lot of Holmer. His peculiar doings went on for a year.

The journalists worked. One had been close to the scene; a man of thirty years experience, he had observed the odd behaviour of people who would come to be identified as members of a particular group well known for extreme right-wing views, outspoken in their hatred of Palme. Described by Holmer as colleagues; creatures a better word. In the face of a mounting body of evidence Holmer, discredited, was replaced by an attorney-general who refused, consistently, to give hearing to any statement that threatened to contradict the official line: all enquiry would be secret, and conducted by the secret police, the Säpo known for detestation of all that Palme stood for. None of these people has been invited to explain himself or to give an account of their movements – the strange presences and also strange absences – before a judge, let alone in public in front of an independent tribunal.

One may conclude that the determination to pursue no path that might lead to police involvement has had the highest political authority. A journalist from *Zeit*, the universally respected Hamburg newspaper, free of tampering, threats or subornation, has named a former Minister of Justice in Sweden, at that time Ambassador in Paris and at that moment unaccountably missing from his post, and whose explanations of this fact have not held water.

"Summing up," Brigitta was saying, "after running it through." Any new light or small salient, before unnoticed in the thicket . . . Mister Charles had, it was true, been full of speed at the time. He'd talked to the journalists, interviewed – or sought to – some of the protagonists, didn't like what he heard. Wrote, yes, a paper for a weekly. Designed a follow-up but his editor . . . 'Climate of opinion, chum, is in favour of spiking this, as thought over-tendentious in Washington. Not sure we've enough of a case to go upsetting them right now.' Lily-livered, but he'd shrugged. He had no particular reputation in investigative journalism, true. John is not a real-ol'-drinking-pal. Just a novelist who does occasional pieces for us.

It was after the fire that John thought of this. So much

had been lost, the raw and the rough of everything he'd ever done: in a way, the whole of a professional working life. The stuff of composition; sediments of – what – maybe creation? Splashes of blood on it sometimes. Is it interesting at all, this process he had been through some forty times? The manuscript notebooks, the in-progress typescripts, the corrections in galley, the niggling at printer's-error in page proof, and the row of finished copies in their spanking-fresh jackets, gone stale on – by now – a long shelf. The libraries of American universities like such things and are ready to buy them. He'd said no. Cathy, perhaps, might like to deal with it all after he was gone. Well, now it was too late and he didn't know whether he felt sorry.

The lots-more, one was only too glad to be rid of: the file-after-file of letters, contracts, clippings, notions: the work shelved and then abandoned; the things that seemed good at the time, hot for a few weeks until enthusiasm pales and among these the 'Palme' file. As documentary it hadn't the legs; the man in Hamburg had done it better, given it the follow-through, but without proper judicial hearings . . . Among the immense mass of fusty, foxy old paper he remembered this biggish folder, of many notes and a few reels of taped verbatims.

Was the timing of the fire a coincidence? Because of the ten-year rule. Right now, this minute, all evidence of conspiracy or collusion among the accomplices in the Palme assassination is no longer valid. But the fire had been before the date. And there's no such thing as coincidence. There are reasons in logic. There are reasons too in what we call metaphysics, for lack of a better word. Not susceptible to what a prosecutor, or a judge, will admit as 'proof'. A great many people won't even accept the existence of the concept.

Had there been in that folder something evidential? It

had been read over, listened to, a score of times. And we all missed it? Such things have been known.

And with this grain of sand, sticking as it were in his digestive process, he had returned here to Brigitta's flat. She is herself no more than a hundred thousand like her; the 'left wing', the 'intellectuals', furious that justice has never been done, and so conspicuously left undone.

He came back to Brigitta, with a jolt. She was speaking.

"One could see half of this discredited and it still leaves a stiff case to answer if we could get it heard – you're looking out of the window again."

"Yes."

"Any interesting assassinations out there?"

"The police could know I'm here. Ya, no passport check on Community people, but I don't know, airline passenger manifest or whatever, if they cared to look."

She would not get into any flap; sturdy; to think herself blackened, even threatened, by my company would amuse her.

"When I argued that these attempts, or feints, at getting rid of you might be genuine if incompetent, you sniffed."

"I'm supposing that the man who got shot would feel it was serious enough. If insane. A house burned down – doesn't that begin to be more serious?"

"If this is so," she said, "then you're at risk here, of anything – being pushed under a tram . . . But John, my dear, have you come here to provoke a showdown? Isn't that unbalanced?"

"To wish to know? And I don't know. Suppose there were in one of those tapes a giveaway, never cottoned on to. I can't get it back since I don't know what it was. But they – might not know that."

"If there ever was anything. You mean the man who went to Chamonix for the weekend, and hadn't?"

"That we might still find proof. They can't feel sure. All that I'm sure of is that if they could track me across France they'd have no trouble knowing now that I'm here." A silence. "I'd better go to bed I suppose. Bit pissed, anyhow. I'll be thinking better in the morning, one always does."

"Do you want me in with you?" asked Brigitta.

The night of February the twenty-eighth passed without any happening worth mention, and so did two subsequent days of quite noisy exhibitionism. And nothing happened. That is a joke, maybe a good one; one does not always see them as funny at the time.

This word 'fun' in English – at best it's ambiguous. Leaving aside funny things that happened on the way to the Forum, people's notions of Aren't-we-having-fun vary, widely. Wearing paper hats, pulling Christmas crackers. Listening to Bruckner. Dancing at Lughnasa. Fun of the fair. Making funny faces. More funny things are planned for me, no doubt. I've been thinking about these. As no doubt I've been meant to.

One scenario could be that I become more disturbed. For as Brigitta has remarked I am getting pretty paranoiac and could become dangerously unbalanced. Dangerous to myself; under a breaking strain people come to think it will be less trouble to make an end of themselves. The police – and this is no coincidence either – quite often find life unbearable, since this is a funny old world. Suicide comes high on their list of hazards, and eating one's own pistol becomes a truism.

Or giving people 'a good fright' – hilariously funny – to be really successful, should end in a cardiac arrest. Why else do people say, 'You frightened me half to death'? If 'to death' they'd hardly be in a position to talk about it. It's quite easy to frighten people to death. The little boy, in

Graham's story, who hid in the dark at the children's party, terrifies us because it happens so naturally; quietly.

The bad detective stories of my youth were full of frights made lurid; the fun-fair effect. Ghost trains, speckled bands, tricks with mirrors, vampires. If you noticed Father Brown hanging about in the vicinity doing nothing, to show a clean pair of heels would be good advice. Nero Wolfe, innocently opening the drawer to count his beer-bottle caps, found a fer-de-lance inside. Nowadays we'd hope the poor beast hadn't caught cold, but giving the reader a big fright was the idea: that's what people enjoy.

My mind turns more to simpler and less obtrusive behaviour. Is there anything easier than fixing the little packet of Semtex under a car? In a parking lot nobody will notice. Bit of adhesive tape, any schoolboy knows how. Weak features of this one – the instability of home-made explosives. Semtex is safer but the police ought to know how to get hold of some. And timing devices; trickier than they appear on paper. Take the minute hand off a cheap watch – but did your hand shake, ever so slightly? Better stick to the old-fashioned device of wiring it to the ignition. Look – whatever – the police may be a crowd of yobbos but here they're not all like Kristiansen and Kvant. They have people too whose hands don't shake. Knowing how to give me a fright. On the third-time-lucky basis, could well be final.

But the fact is that I was for four days under their nose, Brigitta and I enjoying the pleasures that Stockholm in winter has to offer, and nobody as much as looked sideways at me. And now I am back in Germany. I took the car out of the parking lot without my hand trembling, or only a little when I turned the ignition key.

It occurs to me; at my age I am in any case dying, if imperceptibly, very slowly, so that from day to day one will scarcely notice. As Billy Bones remarked, 'Doctors is all swabs,' but they have got clever at prolonging existence: the place is full of centenarians and I hope they're all grateful. This is an expensive business and one of today's nightmares; who is to pay for it all? Themselves? Us? Neither prospect is greeted with unmixed joy.

This necessary dying never has bothered me much. I have resources. One hopes to keep dignity; a steady eye. But now I find myself beginning to resemble Conrad's Nigger. Get on with your dying then (I am paraphrasing from memory) says the old seaman – is it Singleton? We can't help you with that job. Don't make so much fuss about it.

It is trying, the not knowing. We have all to come to terms with it, and most of us do. In my own instance I am getting fidgeted by the thought of somebody gleeful, thinking up ways of being funny.

So here is John; getting on in life but has always thought of himself as a good effects-man. (In French it's 'cascadeur', a vivid word as well as euphonious.) He hasn't had the taste for hair's breadth scapes – Graham lived to a most respectable age and I've always been a bit doubtful about the Russian roulette; he cascaded with uncanny skill – but he's had his narrow squeaks and exciting moments; quite good at getting out of the car before it rolled over the cliff. Will it be comic now to ginger him up a little, giving perhaps a touch of accelerator while he's still a little way from the edge, thinking he has still plenty of time?

I do not, I hope, feel self-satisfied. Precious little reason to be. But I am beginning to go over my past life. In some detail here or there. Rather carefully.

PART FOUR

Love in the Ruhr

The plane touched down at Heathrow, smooth and ample. There was no sensation of being slapped down; without jerk or jolt the turbulent, fussy air became a placid cushiony soil, all very English. Somebody with a microphone, perhaps a pilot, said, "Here we are. Nice and comfy" with no sarcasm: was one 'Home'? Runway lights winked and rippled with a knowing, conspiratorial look saying, 'Safe now; isn't this cosy'. Down here there was no wind, and no snow, but a familiar fuggy London drizzle of welcome and reassurance. When one got out there was instantly an enormous and unmistakable British smell. Even with eyes shut tight this could never be Frankfurt or Atlanta. Sugar, dirt, and strawberry-flavour disinfectant. Could be, can be nowhere else.

While waiting for his case he found he was still clutching a German newspaper as though it were his last link to the known world; threw it at an overfull bin and the headline stared at him sadly, accusingly. The man next door was reading, 'Eddie Raps Mortgage Rates.' Who was Eddie?

They'd sent a car; polite of them. Spanking Mercedes sedan and a smiling driver. There was a piece of motorway. This surely ought to have been the Great West Road, to reassure Poor Old Dad that things were still as they should be. Perivale – Greenford – the tiny houses with tiny people living in them; minuscule washing machines and minia-ture lawnmowers. 'Modern' English architecture ought to mean the Hoover factory. And the memory came back too of the forever-diving girl in the Jantzen bathing suit – immortalised by Anthony Powell: had she already been there in the mid-twenties, for Jean Templer's seduction? A national monument; they should never have dared – but he was being delivered, smooth as golden syrup (did that still exist?) to a deliciously empurpled piece of Harrodian architecture, dim and perfect and full of flowery polite-ness – as long as there were places like this (in Switzerland there were still a few) one would want to be an old lady on (bitterly contested) pension terms: for a few mad moments he seriously considered the thought of ending one's days in a place like this . . . like this; faded gilt mirrors, a smell of sandalwood sachet, polished, mahogany, English furni-ture, a large luxurious sofa facing tall Edwardian windows, and an up-to-date bathroom. On the coffee table there was a large vase of fresh-smelling floristy flowers and a note from his editor saying, 'Hope you enjoy all this – thought it would suit your mood.' And on the walls were English flower-prints. Thanking the good-mannered driver he'd said, "Perhaps it should have been the Jaguar" – this Englishness had still an immense charm as well as dignity. He sat down on the sofa, cross because tears had come into his eyes. On the table was a box, and in it cigars. And in the fridge (which had been given the false front of an Edwardian po-cupboard) were good-mannered drinks. He would make himself comfortable. The only snag was also on the table; a couple of fax messages one couldn't wish away.

You're free for lunch tomorrow so I'll pick you up here, okay? – Jonathan. Very much okay; his agent of long years and an old friend. A 'schedule' from the press girl, saying, *Rather thin but I'm trying to fill this in. You didn't give me much notice!* which was perfectly true; this had been a sudden caprice. She'd done some hasty telephoning because here was another old friend (he still had one or two) – *Unless horrible things happen you're lunching here with me on Thursday – Roger.* An ex-editor now retired; hm, there was a strong feeling about all this that he himself ought to be retired. High time. Lunching with an Old Man, in the Albany, rat-tail English silver, grilled sole, lamb chops, broccoli, good claret and ripe cheese, this had always been very pleasant but had decidedly a Twilight-Fall feel to it. A dinner date with his present editor, at home. In Chiswick and overlooking the river. Also nice, and, one felt, hastily improvised. And hm, two rather grudging-sounding journalists. They weren't exactly rushing, crowding in to greet him, were they now? Well, he had only himself to blame for that. He made himself a big long drink, took a powerful swallow, lit a small cigar, leaned back, closed his eyes.

I have been feeling my heart. I never pay much heed to this; mine is sound. But of course it's a warning sign, saying Slow Down. So I generally equate it with a spell of overwork. This time, a succession of alarms, anxieties. One still has no proper certainties of how real they are. That is generally the picture, isn't it, with a man of seventy? Alerted, you pop in to see The Man, in a quiet, beautifully furnished house (financial-wise there's nothing to match cardiology and the social standing is impeccable). He links you up to a variety of machines, he looks and he listens, he'll do you a few activity tests, exercise bike and such, and at length (he has plenty of time) he sits behind that reproduction of a Louis XV map table, and he smiles and says, Well Now. It's all quite comforting, as it's meant to be: it's when the bill comes in you feel in need of the bypass job.

Brought up on Kipling I find often enough that a line jumps unasked into my petty actuality. It will be so, still, with a few of my generation in England. But we're getting fewer; Roger shuttling gently between the Albany and the Travellers', a winter holiday in Madeira, a summer month in Corfu.

What makes that rear rank breathe so hard? Answer, writing crime fiction. It hasn't quite come to 'What makes that front-rank man fall down?' – I do, to the first, and it will, to the second. But there's also a light-hearted rhyme about the nasty habits of camels. 'What makes the soldier's heart to penk, what makes him to perspire?' My camels are still unidentified, but their detestable character is by now well established. The Swedish police isn't, even if they do behave as badly as that loathed beast. So what is it? These oddities have got to be connected. I don't see how, let alone why. The funny coincidence department can be written off, that's for sure. This last week, in the fine old Roman and Rhineland city of Cologne (bright sun, cold winds) nothing happened at all. I made up my mind that (as had been the purpose of the half-finished plan at Roscoff) I would cross over to England, there look about me; take stock of matters. I am due there anyhow, to burnish the fortunes. Going on as they do, sceptered isle and so forth, Brits have drifted further offshore from mainland Europe than at any time perhaps since Julius Caesar's day: the tunnel provides an ironic comment. The huddle-together syndrome applies most to the over-fifties, precisely those where one finds most readership. One has to repair this: if they don't read about you in the paper you cease to exist. I have been like the little boy, didn't want any nasty soup today, diminishing. A phenomenon which applies also to Brits. So for a few days I Am Brit: let's drink to that.

He stubbed the cigar-butt, drained the glass, closed the eyes; time to get the batteries charged. No further need for the heart to penk; one is At Home.

An editorial interjection is needed here. I myself, the 'Jonathan Wade' here mentioned, am well placed, if by sheer coincidence, to supply it. When I came to read this section of the 'notebook' there was little there of real interest. Most of it had turned into diary notes; about shopping, for instance: John had lost much in the fire, had been living out of a suitcase, and bought a lot of things both to 'build up the morale' and because he could get them here cheaper: in other countries the pound sterling isn't what it was. This, for any reader myself included, is very dull.

Then there is a good deal about personalities, who are alive and who might well take exception to some of the remarks made; often disagreeable. These were nearly all John's old cronies, and in general they'd be tolerant: they still mightn't like their domestic behaviour or scraps of indiscreet conversation thus made public. I ought to know – I was one, and while a grin spread often across my face a few veils had better be drawn. This was the whirl of gaiety; all his meals in restaurants or in private houses; he ate heartily, smoked a great deal too many cigars, and drank enormously – he remarks himself that he was 'permanently pissed', and quite contrary to his permanent habit sleeping late of mornings, both to recover from an unaccustomed social round, and to 'metabolise' immense quantities of hospitable good wine.

I believe there are two points which need making. One

is that he found a sense of anticlimax. He had gone to Sweden and spent a few days with 'Brigitta' (her name has been changed), quite expecting, and one could even say 'hoping' that he had been right to think that unknowingly he possessed some scrap of evidence that would incriminate people implicated (I must choose words carefully) in the assassination of Palme. When this came to nothing, all that electricity, you might call it, wasted, it would be fair to say he felt a sense of nothingness. Cologne is of course a charming city and he has friends there, who deal in art: he didn't want any art. Rushing there to London on impulse, he was in an edgy, captious state of mind.

The second point is that John was always ambivalent in his attitudes towards his own country. This can be traced in a large measure to his childhood, of which I knew little then. It is enough to remark that he was one of the cranky, eccentric Englishmen not at all uncommon, who take a bitter pleasure in rejecting the more conventional English viewpoints and often take refuge in self-imposed exile; both the elder and the younger Philby come to mind. They have undoubted talent, often indeed brilliant; immense charm; are good friends, delightful human beings. And they have bees in the bonnet, which can become obsessive, 'King Charles' Head', for they have a crack in the personality, right down the middle. A phrase that John would jeer at as cliché, but there's no denying the reality. When in England he would show an exaggerated affection for institutions he considered noble, if antiquated, while abounding in fury towards those he disliked, quite harmless features of London life like Hanoverian royalty or Lords Cricket Ground.

I had anyhow an appointment that day with young Matt Arnold (he must have suffered from the name at school but has composed himself to a bland and competent career in publishing); they have two or three of my writers, whom I wished to discuss. It is a highly respectable old house, with rather priggish premises in a listed Georgian building. John has been there for years, for long a valued asset, now rather over the hill. Matt, who is in his thirties, inherited him from the head of the firm, a famous old tyrant now dead, and is a little afraid of John, who hides a natural timidity behind a bullying manner and jokes about 'Spode cups but weak tea'. Inclining thus towards crossness.

"Here's Mister Charles announcing he'll be in our Midst tomorrow, expecting me to have the press bowing on the doorstep, blithely unaware it's unimpressed, since it thought the last three books were Boring. However, we've got him on to Scotty." This guru presides over a television programme, thought to be a feather in writers' hats.

"Oh good. That'll be a distinct help." Matt made a yagh sound.

"Lucky somebody got laryngitis and we popped in on cue. He thought it might be an unexpected field."

"Let's hope John behaves himself, he can be shatteringly rude." I added, "Do your best to be conciliatory."

I had some qualms; this Scotty's quite a decent chap but imbued with a sense of his importance, likes to think himself on the dangerous-edge-of-things, and is a scorer-off. If drunk, which he would be (afraid of being afraid) and tending to fall into a light doze, John would be vulnerable. He affects despisal; however, I needed not to worry.

Scott took irritatingly long with his introduction.

". . . one of our notable exotics, comes drifting in here with a smell of Havanas, so rarely seen one wonders what brings him . . . John, do please look less nonchalant."

"Sorry, I didn't know I was supposed to speak."

"Don't be ridiculous, you're not at the dentist."

"What's this Exotic?" The small prickle would make the man abrasive.

"Isn't there a risk for a writer appearing so seldom, of turning into a purely continental camellia? Highly decorative but lacking in impact?" Showing the bull the cape.

"To be honest, the idea is to read the book, rather than watch the writer picking his nose."

"But are we being quite honest?"

"Everybody suspects himself of at least one of the cardinal virtues, and I am one of the few honest people I have known."

"Sounds like a quotation."

"So it is. Fitzgerald – your namesake."

"You're a great admirer?"

"Writer, and crime writer, very much so."

"Good, let's talk about your definitions of crime writing."

This was quite nice, brisk and even friendly until the man with a tolerant raised-eyebrow face suggested that these were eccentric viewpoints, weren't they? – and dropped the fatal word 'quirky' which won't do.

"'Don't sauce me, in the wicious pride of your youth.'"

"I'm sorry, is that Dickens?" adroitly. John should be sorry!

"I'm not sure . . . perhaps Franz Kafka?" Not sorry. "We'll agree upon a good crime writer." Back payment for the camellias. But without rancour, and at the end, "Thank you, I enjoyed that."

I picked John up afterwards and we had dinner with some journalists: by then pretty far drunk he got a laugh from saying, "One was tempted to ask whether he wasn't perhaps related to Captain Scott, who brought the empire to the Antarctic, wasn't very good at it, went about putting snowshoes on the ponies."

The 'notebook' hereabouts – he didn't date 'entries' but one can often match them to a context – has a dry remark about applause. 'Those bastards weren't thinking me witty – they were laughing at me.' He could have been drunk at three in the morning or sober before breakfast. 'At least one doesn't have to endure the standing-ovation, the spontaneous-outburst rehearsed by the advance man, tough little bugger racing through the baseball stadium yelling, 'Up Up Up, for the Governor'. We only have the publisher's press attaché.' Probably at breakfast: John liked to start the day with a very-large-cold glass of mimosa; would appear downstairs an hour later for the soft boiled egg, a great deal of coffee, and lacking those wonderful German petits-pains, lots of buttered toast. The thing to notice here is that he was frugal when at home-disciplined about drinking. Good coffee whenever I stayed with him, but 'yesterday's bread'.

The next note is apposite; John detested television, refused to appear over the years of his successes, and had only agreed now in the knowledge that his sales had slid a lot.

'One works alone, in a space one tries to fill with light, and generally it is dark. Remember the monks at Maria Laach, the plainsong of Tenebrae on Good Friday. How solitary is the city, that once was full of people. I should be going to parties, meeting good-ladies who say, "Do tell me about your last book, I'm afraid I haven't read it yet." I envy actors, and singers, who merit their applause. A book comes out and one just tries to feel that life is not altogether a mockery.'

At a guess, before even the champagne-and-orange juice.

Nor can I resist the next note, since it is a portrait of myself. 'Jonathan Wade bland bun of tanned pale face always looking just that very second shaved, pale fair hair scanty, arranged to cover a broad scalp, big flat ears that listen well. Trained to show little expression, as becomes an agent. Dressy, check suits of supple material, expensive cut. Old-Etonian voice and manner, used as mask for much kindness.' This sounds as though I were about to appear in a book! I am comforted by the footnote. 'I am deeply fond of this pillar, far from the concept of ten per cent man, no resemblance to Swifty Lazar.'

I took him to the Garrick. Mr Charles feels comfortable in this familiar stamping-ground, where many dead and gone editors have worn the Neapolitan ice-cream tie, told jokes and given excellent companionship. John, the world's unclubbable, feels himself here the Londoner which he was, along-of Mr Fox and Sheridan. He is addicted to marble busts, periwigged men of Distinction engrooved with the dust of King William the Fourth. One orders very large apéritifs, and about a gallon of house claret to follow.

I found dialogue written for me. Enjoyed your performance last night. Next time I see Mr Scott, likely enough standing next door in the gentlemen's lavatory, send a smoke signal. Camellia in the buttonhole? My carnation was arousing John's admiration. He had a small inward disturbance, possibly laughter.

I had to give him a small lecture; people like Scott are there to make the soufflé rise, getting the book talked about. John said Tchaah, not listening. One has to spend a lot of time applying balm to bruised literary egos. John as is his wont gave birth to a bad limerick. Enchanted at getting a blood orange in the vodka.

> "Bright little journalist clot
> Massaging itself until hot.
> The ring of the pot

> *Bright red on it's bot*
> *Locking me into a slot."*

Immediately upon which I got the tirade about crime writers, and not just Kafka or Fitzgerald but the beloved-Graham and a whole lot more. Plus the first Queen Elizabeth the downfall of England, adroit politician playing the nationalist string for all it's worth, ridiculous C of E to back it up, and the severest of state police to enforce it, cut the country off from Europe for good and all. We'll never get back; we've had the odd civilised king but they had to give way to the flood tide of jingoism and xenophobia which has marked us ever since. Perfectly good historical theory and I rather agree but it doesn't do to say so in public. Particularly not at this moment when every Englishman over fifty feels sore and puzzled at our being so third-rate, after all being brought up to believe we were the Best. John's always been Cassandra and naturally they hate his rubbing in the salt.

Parallel to this you have his insistence that no novelist is any good unless it's a crime novelist; since most of our crime books are as wordy as they are worthy he feels a natural dislike and mutters about overpraised mediocrities: so they are and it still doesn't do to say so, since the public isn't anxious to be told yet again that the Spanish do it better.

Lastly of course, the old boy's getting a bit long in the tooth. Should be content; does very nicely and oughtn't allow a dismissive word in the *Bridport Advertiser* to perturb him.

Something else is worrying him and I don't know what it is. Likeliest is a bit of grit in that rather hedonistic existence. Something personal? – a delightful young mistress gone sour on him? Sibylle was in many ways an appalling woman. I always liked her. She was so damned radical; no sense of compromise. Since John has none either it was a foregone conclusion they should end in bitter clash. He's never been willing to admit how much she meant to him, to myself, to himself, to anybody. Be quite sure that he's very lonely. Never a happy situation. The Rogue Male is not just another cliché. I can't do much but apply ointment and hope that an abscess is not forming, painful as well as toxic.

That driver took me seriously! Left a note in the office, good conscientious man, that I preferred to be driven in the Jaguar. So that sailing out, 'leaving Cheyenne', towards Heathrow, I have a moment to think of this triviality; one makes a joke and it's taken seriously (the patriots would feel it their duty to disapprove of Daimler-Benz). The opposite happens also and all too often. Being perpetually on the wrong foot; I am overfull of my own contradictions. One is reminded of Philby (St. John, Philby père; I suspect one would prefer Kim's company). A man perpetually at odds with himself, and at war with his own Englishness; one would be sorry for him, but that would mean my being sorry for myself.

My behaviour while standing about in Heathrow is a case in point; why do the Favourite Airways stewardesses look so untidy and so dirty? Is it only because their uniforms are unbecoming, badly cut and the wrong colour? I was then snubbed by a rude and negligent Air France stew: it serves me right. Mr Kipling put it well, in a delightful *Just So* rhyme for children, about the horror We feel towards They; forever unaware that they

> *'Look upon We as only a kind of They'.*

I am flying on, from Germany. I don't know why I

'decided' this; perhaps that the Oddities, as I think of the Enemy, left me to my own devices while in England. Just as they did in Sweden. So that I have decided to give them a third chance, trying to grasp whether 'the pattern' so far makes any sense.

Also because Cathy is my favourite child. Possibly it would be said that any father has a special relationship with the (only) daughter. Perhaps Cathy is my favourite girl, for all she's the spitting image of her mother. What odds? I loved Sibylle. I still do . . .

I can think of another reason. Of all my children Cathy is the only one who cares about books. Jaimie, while not exactly a fanatic bridge addict, has a strangely mathematical mind: we see each other seldom. We aren't hostile, but there's an unspoken agreement that we have little to say to one another. It's not even unfair to suggest that he's a bit ashamed of me. Alan is a delight, not least because he's so unfailingly kind. And we laugh at the same things. And I get on excellently with his lovely, sharp, and kind Laetitia. Further she does not look, Ever, like an Imperial Airways stew. Still less, one is tempted to say, like the Air France version. (I am high, on a sparkling day, over the North Sea. At least I think so; does one ever know what corridors the toothpaste tubes follow in flight?)

Now Alan is a highly cultivated chap, sharpened and sophisticated – a theatre-goer in three capitals, a picture buyer and a concert fan, the man artists everywhere depend upon. His house is full of books. But a book lover? Not really. Cathy is, though.

(England, bless it, is also full of book lovers. I didn't meet any, alas. We were very professional throughout and talked about marketing the whole time.)

It is another parenthesis, really, but I cannot help thinking of two famous French politicians, both the most terrible crooks, dreadful by any standard of judgment but these; both were most sincerely loved by a great many women, and both were book lovers. One can, and one will, forgive a great deal to both Monsieur de Talleyrand (the family were dukes) and Monsieur Mitterrand (they were the smallest of provincial shopkeepers; have you ever been in Jarnac?). There is a wonderful witness to old Tally in a library. 'He talks to books as though they were alive.' Which of course they are, and Mitterrand did too. That magnificent face, the personification of dishonesty, is also filled with nobility. Tally was just the same.

The thoughts of this nature occupied me; I am skipping of course; my (Lufthansa) plane was skimming in to land near enough to Barcelona. Cathy, who lives and works hereabout, will be here to meet me. She won't let me down; she 'gave me her word'. Like Sibylle, she keeps it. I can rely upon her utterly. I had phoned her from London. 'It's not particularly convenient,' said that clear, low voice, both softer and harsher than Sibylle's, 'but I'll manage, and of course I can put you up.' Cold isn't the right word. Water may seem arctic, but there are fissures far below, from which the earth's heat escapes. This water will be very clear, very pure; yet unexpectedly fertile. Cathy is not married. She has, it is certain, a man. He doesn't live with her. There will be traces of him in the flat, and she will have obliterated them; they are none of my business. Cathy is of course a teacher; dispenses English letters to secondary-school children.

"Hallo."

"Hallo." A small kiss. She is not 'emotional', especially in public. As a little girl she was pretty, vivacious. She fluttered. 'Mariposa' – I was learning Spanish at the time. The last learned, it has been the first to go; sign I'm getting old. My few remaining words will be enough, I thought, listening to the exchange, in Catalan too fast for me to follow, with a policeman discontented with where she'd left the car. I should like to believe I was like Dumas' d'Artagnan – formerly he always wanted to know everything; nowadays he always knew enough. In Cathy's town the cathedral bell was tolling, reminding one of Hemingway, that third-rate fellow (the French admire him; they would . . .) 'Oyó campanas,' said the tart Spanish critic, 'pero no supo de donde' – he heard bells but didn't know where from. Cathy is not like Mister Hemingway.

"You'll want a drink." She poured out some fairly flinty cava, coloured it with a drop of blackcurrant, unsugary; there are people who put in Ribena, don't see the difference but Cathy likes her drinks too to be dry. She sat opposite me in a big cane chair and gave me at last her brilliant smile, stretching her long legs. She is like her mother but leaner, a face of sculpted planes and hollows. Her hair is tawny, a lion colour, cut short but long enough to soften that fine head. The striking feature is the Roman nose. Few people find her beautiful but those that do are emphatic about it and I am among them. Were it merely aquiline she would be distinguished but plain. For the rest, that long figure looks trained and ready, and she has excellent legs. You will gather that I am very proud of my daughter. Spain suits her and she suits Spain. Her balcony looks out upon the landscape of the usual Spanish town, half mediaeval and half cheap barrack. As usual there aren't enough trees. I don't know that I much admire the Visigothic cathedral, with much Jesuitry inside. Franco's troops cannonaded the place, and then they all had a Te Deum Laudamus in the church. It is already warm. Almond blossom is out. We are quite high here in the hills and the air is fresh. Looking at Cathy one understands simple values; that air, earth, water are rare and precious things, which we must fight for. I like Spain much, even if it is too hot for me and there are too few trees. A pity because I like above all this people. I suppose I'm too much of a northerner. I like it that she is happy here. And Barcelona isn't even an hour on the autoroute, and that is not a provincial place.

In the evening sun we stretched, drank our wine, smiled and didn't talk much. I began to unwind.

In England there had been a snobbish, arrogant, intolerant man, full of prejudices, worse, of foibles. Things were very different here. He did not need all those efforts to stay in front, to be English, to be Superior. They have to face humiliations, and his generation has still not got accustomed to these: to being found wanting, in a hundred ways; then they get very petulant. Being condemned, by the Court in Strasbourg; being told off by the neighbours for polluting the sea or not having any social legislation. So many blows to our pride, it's like losing all the Test Matches to a pack of Wogs. So we wrap ourselves in a fit of the dignities, turn still further inward, start yattering about that moth-eaten sovereignty. I am just the same.

Here the himself was a simpler man, and he hoped a better one. Getting to be old, he hoped not too smelly. Getting weary. Catherine's look is full of affection, for her father whom she knows, likes, loves. And respects. This gives her the right to be cutting, where it is needed. And Cathy-Booklover, a widely read one, a good judge. Jaimie would say, 'Haven't read it. Sorry, don't intend to. A goodish writer, leastways I've always supposed so.' Ashamed of his father, but not on that account. Alan would have taken a quick look, enough for an intelligent comment, enough to mask the not-caring-much. His father is a writer, that's good – if it comes to that a good enough writer to be proud of if pushed. Socially acceptable; it's an honourable trade. But Cathy reads them. Has a shelf of them there, if he didn't send her a complimentary copy she'd go out and buy it. She'll say, 'This is good; that isn't.' With her he is at ease. (Sibylle took on the whole a poor view of writers, and that included him.)

"Do you want a shower, while I'm cooking? Give me your underthings and I'll throw them in the machine with mine." I had forgotten that she can be tryingly managerial.

"What's this? Mr Pepys – I've never read him."

"Immensely civilised. 'Lord, to see the absurd nature of Englishmen, that cannot forbear laughing and jeering at everything that looks strange.' Lovely man."

"Can I have him to take to bed with me?"

"He'd have enjoyed that." In her bathroom one is conscious of her femaleness; cosmetics, tampons and things lying about. I had never seen her in this light, even when she has stayed with me. I am not calmed in a sedation sense; I feel a serenity through my whole being. What is that place? – where Luther came from – is it Fulda? They have a fine church. Outside it has a massive, fortress-looking tower and written round this in huge red letters 'EIN FESTE BURG.' What I need.

And in my honour – "I don't cook much as a rule; bit of fish, y'know, with risibisi" – she had a real Spanish stew, cocido with beef and beans and cabbage, and lots of potatoes, lots of juice from a marrowbone; did me good; 'me too, change from all that salad' and a thirty-year-old Rioja 'from my man', she said equably.

Her 'advice' is the same, oddly enough (why odd? – nothing odd about it), as Brigitta's was. If this is your fate accept it. The northern woman had seen a winter journey, through the medium of Schubert's song cycle. These mountains, these frozen rivers; the journey is through oneself. Cathy nodded, added a half-forgotten fragment from the poem by Hardy about Napoleon in Russia.

> *"'This snow, this sky,*
> *Soldiers, it is I'*

"Something like that. You know, I'm on your side. While of course I'm not on anyone's side."

It was his turn to nod. She had also been on her mother's side.

"You were harsh. Cruel even. Oh, I don't mean to us children." Like Alan, she added, "We had, I think, a balanced, a happy childhood. But to Sibylle, needlessly so. You could be so cutting, so wounding. Artists are like that. I know. They'll stop at nothing in defence of their essential central being. Makes them impossible to live with. I should know." Was it a corner lifted on her own past, or was it just being his daughter?

"You were shockingly demanding. She was very patient, you know."

"She could be shocking herself. A nice line in insult. You'll agree that she was exasperating. Provoked one past endurance. One day driven bats I said, Oh, Fuck Off, and quite coolly she said, 'I wouldn't mind being fucked by someone who knew how to do it' – I was really taken aback."

Cathy was quite unmoved. "You ought to know, or you're a poorer psychologist than I take you for, how adaptable women are, how quick and skilful at using a man's vocabulary and turning his own arguments against him."

"I do know. But it was so unlike her."

"She learned from you."

"Look – do you know of anyone who wants to assassinate me?"

"I hardly think it would be my mother." Unsmiling and indeed unhumorous. "Some instinct, nothing more, tells me that there's a woman behind this. That's all."

"I'll have to search further then. I haven't all that wide a past acquaintance."

"Do so," woodenly. The jungle, as the fellow said, is neutral.

At breakfast, wonderful and his best time of day, Cathy had gone out for fresh rolls, and giggling – 'Something I don't know what to do with' – put on the table a twee little wooden shelf with six dainty pots of jam.

"Up came the minesweepers – 'Claribel, Assyrian, and Golden Gain.' Happily; to have slept very well is rare enough now to be a win.

"Really they are awful." She was 'ashamed'.

"Russian-roulette jam, five will be inoffensive and the last contains a mortal dose of cyanide."

She has to go to work, and he – he's on holiday; what a nice thought. He has been told to do nothing, but he will enjoy this scrap of housekeeping: the unpacking of the dishwasher, the polishing and putting-away of glasses, the making-up of aired bedclothes, a little languid dusting, chasing crumbs with the vacuum-cleaner – it's like being married to her. One will then sit, with as good a conscience as though he had been working . . . a fourth cup of coffee and Read the Paper. Turning the political pages of *Vanguardia* in a lordly awareness of not having to bother; one knows all that already.

An amused comment on petty-doings; the tenor Pavarotti (who is sixty if a day and not known for nothing as Fat-Lucy) has been asinine enough to play with young girls, and his wife has had to choose her wording with some care when interviewed.

'When the evening of one's life arrives,' the Italian put into Spanish is coming out in a stiff and pompous English, 'the sensation of solitude which overcomes successful men needs to be fought with the help of long-lasting, rooted, confirmed sentiments.' A dignified statement, and in Italian better still. He put down the paper.

Weren't these his sentiments, expressed often and sometimes at much greater length towards a stubbornly stone-faced wife? In English mostly since this had been from the start the language of their life together. Defensible; it was the language of his working existence. But it could be in French: 'Quand vient le crépuscule . . .' Or in German, for when she got at all worked up, it was in her native, supple and vigorous tongue that she . . . and of course he can speak German; competent enough, even quite workmanlike. 'Wenn das Abend . . .' He'd never progressed beyond his original level – never had learned genders; three like in Latin but that's at least one too many. A fair vocabulary; Abendrot, a sunset, Dämmerung, the twilight. Germans tended always to rock with laughter, whereas he'd spoken French since childhood. In any language the accent – but so what? 'Would it sound better if I talked with a Corsican accent? Or plat-Bayerisch?' Sibylle, with her Rheinland voice, always made it sound pretty.

Look, girl, these thirty years and more. Repeating it hadn't made it the more convincing. We have had bad times but we have always Maintained. Isn't that worth something, even a lot? We have held to fidelity, loyalty, honour; we have brought up three children, and not badly either.

He had found it convincing; she had not. Pious Christian sentiments, she had said in a cool unemotional voice.

As placidly immovable he found Cathy now.

"Having the same squaw for thirty years isn't a medal to

115

pin on your chest. You wanted – you needed, it wasn't your fault – a squaw and you got a very good one. She then decided there had to be more than that in her life, and she was quite right. I had to admire you at the time because you saw the basic justice of it and you didn't complain. Don't do so now."

"Do you see something of her?"

"Those are my affairs, and I see no need to discuss them. Would it be nice if I made some soup?"

"Let's go into the town together. Let me take you out and give you dinner; allow me to be proud of my pretty daughter."

"I'll put on a frock. I smell of unwashed teenagers."

That night he did not sleep well.

Cathy brought him to the plane, 'being kind' all the way, insisting upon carrying his little case (all his things washed and ironed), kissing him affectionately at the barrier, saying how lovely it had been, waving energetically like a mother with a little boy setting out for school; why had he this sinking feeling? As though sure that he would never see her again, any more. In a plane (even this early full of German tourists scratching their sunburn, breath laden with alcohol and offensively jolly) with a nun next door to him saying her rosary, the boarding-school feeling remained strong.

A night of waking and sleeping, neither to be distinguished from the other, and the dream in the last five minutes, telling oneself to get up, for otherwise one will be late for school.

They told me I was going to be shot. I was alone, far from help; sitting, perhaps lying?, on a bare stone floor. I was resigned to it; I do not remember being frightened. Some vague curiosity; was it to be Chinese, that economical method of bringing one out into the crowd (edifying spectacle) between two soldiers, quite friendly, support-ing one rather than brutal, fumbling then for the pistol, cocking it, did one feel the cold metal of the muzzle on the nape of the neck? The inventive touch is to send the bill for the bullet to the family; I pictured Cathy tearing open the envelope, making a face, tax-collector again.

No, it was Spanish, a bare yard between walls of massive, mediaeval masonry; more casual, a chore to be done like polishing one's boots. A few soldiers sitting on steps clean-ing their equipment, smoking; one shambled across with the fag still in his mouth to where a machinegun stood on a tripod; he went down on one knee, swung it to aim, closing one eye as though to wink at me. I can remember the shock of the bullets hitting my chest, having time to think, 'That's it,' before blacking out – it was not dread-ful. I remember even thinking, 'Sloppy, wasteful – more than half those bullets will hit the wall and I hope they don't send the bill to Cathy.' All easy-going, quiet and businesslike. They said nothing that I recall. I had a moment to recollect myself. Didn't shout or wave my arms, like in the Goya picture. Nor take my hat off and say 'Soldiers!' like Marshal Ney. Just stood there, shambling and idiotic.

Firing-squads cost too much money – the Administration sent an instruction that they be stopped.

Dreams fade quickly as a rule: why did this linger, dis-agreeably? To quieten it he took Mr Pepys from his pocket. 1664, honesty, lechery, hypochondria.

In the seat behind him two biddies with penetrating voices Germanly discussed the merits of their respective diar-rhoea remedies. The trouble seemed to be that you know how it is, dear, you're taking your usual pills, not to speak of indigestion, hangover, and the damn Spaniards making such a racket all night, and taking pills for everything, I mean to say, dear, where d'you stop? The holy nun, eyes placidly closed, knew also how to close her ears. He began to compose a schoolboy rhyme.

> *Mr Pepys said, What rot!*
> *I can fart terrifically,*
> *Piss prolifically.*
> *Poop can I not!*
> *But once placed upon the pot,*
> *Well stuffed with pease-porridge hot*
> *(or cold, I wot)*
> *One should hope to begin to trot.*

A prim voice said, "We are now beginning our descent upon Köln."

And now here it was fearfully hot. Gott! After months of ghastly blasting polar wind out of the north, snow everywhere, Glatteis on all the roads, the spring was bloody beaming down inexorably, and a great deal of dusty particles floating in every bloody beam. Lot of road-drilling much as usual, shrill stink of cement, car miles away, also as usual, a long hunt. Where he had left it, above ground (like the poppy just-a-little-white-with-the-dust), impossibly hot and smelly. He sat in it for some time. Tired, aching. Loose too around the bowels. Frightened. Here he was, back in Germany, and for no reason at all suddenly again frightened.

He sat too long; the police came to a conclusion. Heavily loaded down with electronics, fire-power, crowd-control; only the dog was missing. The tread purposeful, weighty with decision, like we were going to squeeze in another cup of coffee before going off duty, but this will do instead. Majestic; handsome, if coarse of feature. God made them, male and female made he them, two of a kind. Went to opposite doors, just in case it were a funny-bunny. The female one tapped on the window.

"Would you mind?"

One can make a to-do. Their search-and-seizure powers are ill-defined, can be challenged, and maybe in court one will triumph, but can one be bothered? Easier to comply, or is that the story of one's life? He had a friend in the police (not here though). Supposedly French, ex-PJ officer, with succinct advice to offer. Never, never have anything to do with them, unless of course you're fucking forced to. And then no rebellion, no sarcasm, just go along, however silly; in the long run you'll waste less time. They only want to be Quite sure you aren't a terrorist, dealer in narcotics, illegal immigrant. You were, you know, Loitering.

"Just putting on the ventilator, you know, wait for the temperature to come back to breathable." It might have been a help, he would think that evening, if they had taken me in, instead of a great telling-off for leaving the motor running. 'Embarked,' as the French police say (charming word for a disagreeable experience), one would have been safer.

"Where are you heading?"

"Arnsburg." It really was the first name that came into his head. It didn't have to be true; they would have been satisfied with anything.

"Very well then – there is your road – past Dusseldorf, direction Hagen – on your way." Lucky to escape the summons for pollution, redeemable by a heavy fine? The car had French plates? He looked harmless, old? He had been humble? And the road – the road leads to a town he had known well in the old days. That had led to Sibylle. Then it was all half-cleared bomb sites, with the first tiny shoots of new life beginning to show, like the first snowdrops beside a soot-blackened trampled icy path through the wreckage. But basically the same path; the road leads to the

Ruhrland. To Dortmund, Essen and Wuppertal. The names of the minesweepers! To Bochum, Oberhausen and Gelsenkirchen – 'Claribel, Assyrian and Golden Gain.'

Arnsburg lies outside the immense industrial nexus. Even today these roads are a surprise. By hearsay one would picture it all as the same grim sprawl with nothing to show ends or beginnings. One is taken aback to find a country of sharp-pitched hills, thickly clothed in pine trees, bare outcrops of rock, steep narrow little valleys where one can trace the beginnings of two centuries before, when the mill was run by water power. Village roofs climb the hillsides, and in the middle a church perched with a high humped nave and a needle spire pointing up to God, and a churchyard full of simple faith and piety. Between Dortmund and Unna there are ploughed fields and solid roomy farmsteads where cows graze. Fierce village loyalties were to 'the mill', where one's father, one's grandfather, through all time . . . oneself went in to the mill as a matter of course at twelve, at ten years old. John, the raw boy, eighteen in the last year of the war, had never seen the Yorkshire mill towns. The pattern is just the same; here you go down the mine; in this valley it's coal. There it's iron, and you make steel: jump one further and you're in the textile country that stretches up into Belgium, over into France to Roubaix and Tourcoing, but be the local language German-French-or-Polish we all understand it.

Climb the hill and you are among cowslips and the slender pallor of the wood anemone.

And here in 1946 soldiers, boys homesick for Barnsley or Workington, lifted singing voices in a sentimental tune nigh as constant as Lili Marlene herself –

That's where I fell in love where stars above –
came out to play –

South of the Border –
Down Dusseldorf way . . .

And so had he.

Today the residential roofs have crept ever further like the lava on the slopes of Etna. It is the mills that stand desolate with pine seedlings growing from the tops of the tall magnificent chimneys. Swing out past Hagen and you are already in Iserlohn. You are following the Ruhr – a peaceful, winding little country river – upstream, to rustic, cow-and-colza origins. Arnsburg lies within a loop of the Ruhr, just south of Wickede. John had turned off the autobahn, for old sakes' sake.

A mistake, this; of course the countryside would have changed, and over fifty years out of all recognition, but he had trusted his memories of the roads between villages, so often travelled he had known them by heart. Sentimentalist idiot, he was now astray, and signs pointing to once-familiar names made his path the more confusing: hereabouts they were cutting a new autobahn and roadworks forcing him to take a big loop northward. A once-famous name on an arrow – there at least he would know where he was. Woods made it invisible from the ridge but the road wound downhill and abruptly he stopped the car at the lakeside; his heart was beating noisily. The Möhnesee . . .

It was now a weekend playground. A couple of comfortable-looking hotels with glassed verandas, a rash of little beer gardens and Boats-for-hire notices. But there in the distance, the massive wall . . . He got back into the car to drive the five minutes along the lake shore and there it loomed up large. They had put it all back, in its monumental fortified Kaiserstyle of the 1900s, with the watchtowers and pretend-mediaeval gateways, and now there was a café selling ice-cream and crisps. Curious, he went to look. Surely there would be a memorial plaque, and perhaps postcards, with photographs of the ruins; as it was in 1945. There was nothing, and John smiled at their talent for obliterating the disagreeable.

"Didn't the Brits" – falsely naïve – "bomb it or something?" The man was in his forties; uninterested.

"That's right. Knock it all down – Springbomben, oder."

And standing here as a green little boy of a junior officer, John had seen a thoughtful figure, walking slowly with a silver-mounted stick. He had straightened up and saluted; it was a Wing Commander, unknown to him but 'there were a lot of them about.' An impressive one; pilots' wings, a double row of medal ribbons, diagonal stripes of a DFC. God knew what he was doing here but such people were a law unto themselves.

"Good morning, sir."

"Morning, boy," morosely.

"Come to see for yourself, sir? Your own work, perhaps?"

"What? That? Dambusters!" With an immense contempt, and a startling bitterness. It would be prudent to keep quiet. The 'Dambuster' Squadron had been one of the great propaganda successes and a lot of clouds-of-glory, and some fine feathers, floated about those concerned. Like 'Pathfinder', about which myth collected. As a very young Pilot Officer (no wings, and no medals either) one took care, and John was silent. The 'old man' (forty perhaps but greying under his cap as many of them had) said nothing but looked at the immense, impressive ruin. Then he pointed his stick at John.

"Boy, let me tell you something. They tried to knock it down and couldn't. Lot of heavies here in the mud at the bottom. They found a guru, one of those dam' scientists. Made them a thing, spherical thing – would bounce, like a bloody pingpong ball, on the surface, run along, hit the dam, and bang."

Yes, it was here. The Möhneseestaudam. A year or so later they would make a highly sensational sentimental movie, with Leslie Howard or somebody (no, not him, he got killed in the war) in the role of the Miracle Scientist.

Nasty pale grey, hard eyes the old man had.

"Just imagine, boy, if you can. How much money, how many millions, d'you think, they spent on developing a thing like that? Think about it. And then the risk, coming in low over the water," pointing, with the stick. "What for? Great success," with crude sarcasm. "Breach this big thing, deprive the civilian population of drinking water. A mighty blow at morale, they called that.

"Now I'll tell you one of my heroic episodes, back in 'forty that would have been, flying some bloody awful crate, dropping propaganda leaflets hereabout, don't believe all Haw-Haw tells you, that sort of crap. Got flak, as was to be expected, some boys started saying Fuck-this, instead of scattering the papers began heaving them over in packets, quite heavy, may be twenty kilo at a time. That leaked out – as such things will. We got torn off a considerable strip for endangering a civilian population which was not, repeat, Not, the assigned mission. We took some pride, boy, then, in waging war. It was a Crusade. We were civilisation, out to stop the barbarians. And look at us now . . . Remember what I've said, boy." Turning, walking slowly away.

A monstrous shock to poor silly John. He would get accustomed to this sort of cynicism. By 'forty-seven, it was commonplace among the seniors; those who really had flown, over Germany. And those in the ranks, too, who had armed and loaded Lancaster bombers. The principal emotion felt by then was shame, and the tough exterior assumed scarcely bothered to mask it. Back in the Mess . . .

John knew his way, now, from here. The road through the woods still led to Arnsburg. The 'Mess' had not been there, but there had been – never mind, it was salutary, to retrace these steps, to call up these disjointed memories, which would tell him, at least, part of what he wanted to understand. For that, he had to relive whatever was still possible, from fifty years ago . . .

He stopped for a bite to eat, in Neheim-Hüsten; two villages now the one prosperous township (the autobahn piercing an underpass, at the bottom of the hill). Weird – a town of old women, and how many of his memories would they share – walking slowly, with sticks in the sunlight, towards the chemist's to have their prescriptions filled: he wanted his own prescription renewed but it would take more than a Pharmacy to decipher this faded palimpsest.

All along the valley and the railway line were strung out depressed fragments of industry, like grey, never-quite-clean washing pinned to rusty wire. But everywhere on the slopes, in orderly lines as neat as freshly pruned and raked vineyards, suburban housing climbed, trim with fresh paint and toy gardens. 'I've gone wrong again,' – and at that moment an arrow caught his eye. Arnsburg Altstadt, and he was climbing through narrow hairpins and this one he knew; this was as familiar as though he'd never been away: will Barbara still be alive?

Nothing suburban up here. This was Urbs, as it had been for centuries, and the Neumarkt a square of quiet dignified old houses, the heart of a traditional, historic German town. Even in 'forty-six it had looked much the same; take away a few gaudy shopfronts. Bombs had fallen here but scattered, indiscriminate; a plane that had lost its way, flustered by flak – or a fighter after it. Unload quick, and get out of here. The gaps had been restored, lovingly. He left the car here; he knew his way. Cross and turn left, going on up the hill. The Altmarkt, cobbled as it had always been so that horses should not slip. these were really old, fifteenth century, trim and fresh-painted in their primitive, childish colours and the gothic lettering of prayers, blessings and conjurations against disaster (an intensely pious God-fearing people) lovingly kept up. The old Rathaus, emblazoned with the splendid, immensely complicated and elaborate arms of the prince and his city, quartering half the ruling houses of Germany and carrying the Wittelsbach label. And the New Schloss, dignified and unpretentious, now the Sauerland Museum.

He had to go on; memories crowded here, pressing on nerve points in his head, wakening sharp jolts of pain. The Schloss Strasse, steeper, narrower, through the Glockenturm gateway. Pleasure? He had taken Barbara up here, the first night. Up there at the hill top, in the bushes around the ruins of the mediaeval castle, the Old Schloss, he had peeled off pathetic and unresisting underclothes. Too steep now for the old man; he stopped to gaze at a lovely crooked house, brave in bright blue and gold lettering – 'Burned down and restored by Michael (baker and brewer) and Maria-Sybille, 1975.' A magnificent view, the valley and the hills across it.

In the lazy quiet of afternoon spring sunshine he pottered, lighting a cigarette and enjoying it. There was nobody about. A little boy rode a bicycle gleefully down the hill; one or two cars were parked in angles of the little old houses. They'd be worth a lot now. He was smiling, amused at the power of this antiquated nigh-instinctive pull of memory that had dragged the old man, breathless now from the hill – or from sentiment – all the way up here. 'Gunther's house' was lower down, out of sight and he would keep it so. There, he had no wish to sentimentalise over the old days. A mistake, no doubt, to have come here at all. He would finish the cigarette, stroll back down – really it had been the spring sunshine, still a novelty this early in the year – climb in the car, sail back towards Essen. *Fidelio* was playing in the Opera and one might have a shot at a ticket. This had been an indulgence. One said to the police 'Arnsburg' – could just as well have been Essen – and then one felt, superstitiously, obliged to make it come true . . .

And then it happened. Not at all surprisingly, all things considered. And as he had pictured that it would happen. Not even fast, and he had imagined that it would be fast and violent: even the violence was leisurely, unhurried.

A car came up, through the gateway, slow and careful, reversed and turned. Day-dreaming – stepping, scrupulous, on his cigarette end – he noticed only an old Mercedes model, shabby and in need of a wash, like his own. The vaguest of impressions of two youngish men. It stopped abreast of him and a man got out, exactly as one would to ask some tourist question, polite and confused. 'Can't one get further, on this path?' Or 'Isn't the museum open?' He was even opening his mouth to say, 'No, it's a dead end.' And then he got a sharp push, in the back. Bundled or barged into the open doorway so that he fell off balance across the seat; he could not struggle and was too taken aback to cry out. His neck was gripped in the crook of somebody's elbow, and as he gasped for breath a pad of cottonwool came down upon his nose and mouth. It reeked of ether. Nobody uses it now as an anaesthetic. One can buy it in any pharmacy. It attracts no attention. An old, simple, household product, used – if at all – to disinfect the skin. Much like hydrogen peroxide. A lot of people don't mind the smell.

I suffered intensely. I was helpless, with an arm pinned under me and the other gripped, my head pushed down in a man's lap and my legs doubled up against the car door. I dread and detest ether, for as a child I was held down brutally by nurses and anaesthetised by this abominable method.

When I came to I was sick. I vomited, several times, and my vomit smelt of ether and this made me retch, helpless. Someone had spread a coarse towel under my jaw. When, at long last, I was finished I was exhausted. My whole body ached. The joints were turned to water. "Go to sleep, now," said a voice, and I did.

What can one make of these half-worlds; sleep and his brother? I have been dreaming; am now awake. Alive. Testing it by touching things. To be alive is no achievement but it's a fact, to be noticed, perhaps thought of; the more since I have readied myself for death. So one should. At my age one thinks of death, of dying suddenly. By violence, but any death is a violence. To sleep and not to wake: will one know one's moment? Readied one will still cling. I have just thought of the young witch, in *The Lady's not for Burning*. A theatre, in London, that year following the war. She said, 'I am such a creature of habit; I had quite got into the way of living.' I am not young, nor pretty, but I agree, the habit is hard to shake.

Why (now that I am certainly awake) this memory, of that year? An evening at the play, and a good one. The still young John Gielgud and the very young Richard Burton: which of them delivered the line I should like to have written? – 'Always fornicate between clean sheets, and spit on a well-scrubbed floor.' I don't much look like doing either right now. Alive, though.

He did little that first day but lie there (between clean sheets). Suffering from shock as he supposed, as well as from unpleasant after-effects of primitive anaesthesia in very likely an overdose.

His watch had disappeared, among other things. Towards evening, by the light, a young man came in. One of the two?

"Want something to eat?" Neither 'kind' nor the contrary.

"Not really."

"Better have some soup." He had brought a bowl, and a spoon. A sort of German minestrone. Smelt nice; a lot of work, to eat it, but he kept it down, felt better for it. Began feeling dozy again. Had there been a sleeping pill dissolved in that? Likely enough.

Born in 1927 John was 'called up' for military service at the war's end. One felt a little humiliated about this. Elders, instructors, disagreeable sergeants with Africa and Italy ribbons on their battledress, tended to rub it in, inventing disciplinary chores for these lucky-little-devils: the expression 'Get yer knees brown' was heard a good deal. Most of these seniors were soured at their own demobilisation being held up, beyond as they felt the call of duty. With the general unwinding of tension and loosening of administrative screws came confusion, muddle and a slackening of discipline; a lot of what-the-fuck, and 'Let the sprogs look after it'. Perhaps for this reason most of John's early months were spent in 'bullshit camps', a great deal of square-bashing, heavy emphasis on boots and haircuts, and 'If it moves salute it' (if it don't move paint it). The feeling of a world become meaningless was widely shared.

John had opted for Air Force service largely though filial piety; his father was dead of some vague cardiac affection but Robert had been in the RFC in the 'last war'. From what one gathered this was still worse than the Army. Many months were lost in a Radio School learning about Wireless Transmission. The service was far-flung; one dreaded getting sent to some ghastly hole in PaiForce, formerly known as Mespot. Officially there were still fleets of bombers, squadrons of fighters, held in readiness for nobody quite knew what.

Saved from all this by the onset of migraine headaches John found himself grounded, downgraded, regrouped, whatever all that might mean ('Some clerk in Innsworth'), posted to Transport Command and sent to administrative duties, whatever that . . . in Germany. He remembered standing clueless in a hangar at Lyneham while a horrible corporal left dirty fingerprints on a mass of paper. Other sufferers had their arse posted to Istres, Fayid, Castel Benito. "Not you, wrong bloody plane, other there then."

"You for Germany? Arnsburg – where the fuck is that then?"

Nobody had ever heard of it. John would wonder, often, about that clerk at Innsworth who had been told to find a junior officer for administration in Arnsburg and had picked on 'Charles, J.' presumably with his eyes shut. He could just as easily have gone to Castelbloodybenito, which was somewhere near Tripoli.

There were a lot of these little ex-Luftwaffe flying fields which had guarded the eastern flank of the Ruhrgebiet. Some were virtually in the city, others crammed into a bit of flat land between hills. Some were closed with a perfunctory bulldozer, bit of barbed wire, or marked 'Unserviceable'; others held mysterious little units on guard duty over obscure 'stores'. Several different Commands were involved. The Squadron was up north of Werl but a lot of ancillary junk was scattered about and here in a loop of the Ruhr were we, supposed to be holding it all together. Around here there had always been big houses. Rich industrialists had built, on the hillsides for the view, vied with each other for the length of the bar. Vulgar villas with swimming pools, a few fine old houses. A lot we cared, confiscating anything delectable we wanted.

This one had come with-the-rations, being a former Jewish property; the Mess in a pretty mansion, other ranks in huts in the pretty park, its trees and grass scored and scarred by careless airmen. In the house lived some thirty officers, sometimes more, in transit to somewhere else, and in the huts perhaps sixty 'erks'; maybe a hundred, and all of it a ramshackle bunch. Lying here in this bed, John found his memories of this world assembling into astonishingly vivid fragments. Minute sketches, which in a writer's mind will dissolve and reform into minor – absurd – characters. Like Len in the guardroom, probably the most unsuitable candidate for the Military Police ever yet thought of. Tall, very fair, broad, blue-eyed and blank, his snowdrop helmet sacramental on the spotless table, his benevolence could not be hidden by an expression of permanent harassment, and he spent most of the day in his underpants ironing the crease in his trousers, his blancoed belt and gaiters put to dry on the windowsill.

Flight-Sergeant Lafferty – everything that poor Lenny was not. He never seemed to do anything, but knew to a hair's breadth and at any moment what everybody else was doing. He belonged, one must suppose, in the Orderly Room but was to be found in anyone else's office and generally the Commanding Officer's, filing and polishing his very clean fingernails. His battledress was threadbare, with a chestful of improbable medals from Aden or Afghanistan. His looks were saturnine, satanic. Rumour clung to him; that in reality he was high in Field Intelligence; that he was the unquestioned king of the black market; that he held blackmail material over the Air

Officer Commanding. His visible power was over all leaves and permissions (of immense complexity, including illicit weekends at 'Home'). His sad sneering face seemed to keep the worst sarcasms for himself, perhaps while looking at those intolerably knowing eyes in a mirror while brushing his teeth. A quiet, hoarse voice, like a rasp on soft wood, in which to be, one has to say, extremely funny. Veiled contempt was often kept for –

Mr Morley, the Station Warrant Officer, a figure of fun with an astonishing music-hall accent. 'Old Joe's on the fiddle, ey? I'll 'ave 'im, I knows all the fiddles, I been 'ospital cook in 'Alton, twenty year.' Joe was the other Warrant rank, the Catering Officer, a bear-like, soft-walking (his feet hurt) man who was of course on the fiddle; everybody in Catering always was. Food (we ate lavishly and well) was distributed to outlying units in a complicated bureaucratic manner from Squadron (Joe went daily, with a three-tonner) which must have helped keep his turpitudes out of the claws of Lafferty. Joe liked to distribute small bribes to the deserving. ' 'Ere's yer rations, chum,' producing a banana from the stomach of his blouse. Accompanying, as Orderly Officer, a CO's inspection, John was charmed when the old gentleman raised his eyes from a well-scrubbed tiled kitchen floor to complain about cobwebs on the ceiling (the hot summer of 1947). 'Well, sir,' said Joe, 'they 'elps to keep the flies down, that's undeniable.'

You must recall that HM Forces had too much of everything, while in the early days at least, the German population had nothing. Soap, blankets, cigarettes or shoe polish vanished at a glimpse, and first and foremost food, since one bought a girl for a tin of Carnation Milk. The cooks were a law to themselves; their 'billet' gleamed with floor polish and was decorated with flowers lifted from the local cemetery – the Rheinland Catholics do not fail in devotion to their dead. Corporal Boswell, shortly to be Sergeant, i.c. Airmen's Mess, was one of the splendid old queens frequent in the regular Army who refer to everyone as 'She'. Catching sight of John one evening when 'out drinking' in Arnsburg, in the company of Barbara, Boswell exclaimed audibly, 'Ow, will you just look at that. Diamond Lil, out with a woman!'

Why have I gone into so much detail? This life of a very green and very junior officer in the Occupying Forces during the immediate post-war years was neither interesting nor exciting. Going this far is to illustrate, and bring in to relief, two essential points. The second, and the real one, is the close and complicated relation of John with Germany, and the Germans. To make this the more understandable, some further light needs to be shed upon the first: the establishment described, while perhaps unusually eccentric, was not untypical either of those odd, forgotten days. To make this clear, just a couple more anecdotes will be brought out.

A Pilot Officer is of course a worm. Tucking in, the first night in a room with Flying Officer Bridgeman, morose soul a year senior to himself, John remarked, "They've given me a fellow called Hammond as Batman; d'you know him at all?"

"He isn't a batman, so you can save your half-crowns. He's a GD; they all are, here." The Aircraftman-General-Duties was, I suppose is, the lowest form of RAF life: to this encampment had drifted much of the lees of the wine. A few over-senior bods who knew their job but sought the quiet life; like Boswell (who once a fortnight made the most marvellous yeast-risen currant buns) or LAC Harvey of the Motor Transport, whose promotion had been blocked by a stiff dose of the Syph in India, which lent him much prestige.

The Officer's Mess was on similar lines, and the little greeny did well to keep quiet there, and never be heard. In the great demobilisation panic a lot of old, very senior, but tarnished wartime heroes, downgraded medically, often burned or crippled, had been held back to form the 'cadre' for a new generation. People disappeared, were never seen again, like the officer encountered by the MöhneSee; 'in transit' no doubt. John's own Commander was just such another and as silvered, as DSC'd and DFC'd, the disillusionment less openly spoken. But in the Mess of an evening – hard drinkers, these veterans, a dozen looking older than their years, wearing Pilots, Navigators, Engineers wings and rows of medals, one did not forget that they had flown the furthest, the most dangerous raids, nor that ghosts walked in their company. After much whisky they would remember their boyhood, break into ironic song.

'We're marching Against England – England by the Sea' and a drumming boot and fist chorus of 'Sieg – Heil – Sieg – Heil'. A drink or two more and one noticed that shame was what they all felt most. There were better ways of serving the King than to turn historic towns into heaps of rubble. An evil precedent set by an enemy does not cease to be evil when copied and multiplied. Nor, as we all knew by then, had depriving thousands of food and shelter lessened an industrial capacity to wage war.

Of course there were dissenters, the Do-it-again-Tomorrow ones, prominently a fat squadron-leader who had commanded parachute-folding, some said shoe polish. Voluble one evening in adumbration of spacious days: the CO, morose over his drink, stirred.

"Shut up, Broadbent, we know that all you ever did was fill in bomb craters." A crushing silence and John saw the barman and the waiter, both hard boys from Glasgow, exchange winks.

"You didn't talk like that on the apron at Tangmere," said the fatman, hotly.

John remembered idiotic passages in his training – the R/T procedure, the hunting-horn jargon of Fighter Command in 1940. 'Flash your Weapon' – 'My weapon is bent' – the cheerful obscenities. Momentarily one saw the tired old man, grey-skinned, the fine eyes now red-veined, again the dashing young flier, silk scarf and hair needing cutting.

"About that fifteen-hundredweight which Harvey says is u/s –" said the Adjutant tactfully.

Why, even the Air Officer Commanding – a figure surrounded by myth; it was said that he kept a personal Spitfire for 'going home in the afternoons' and that he had swapped it for a Messerschmitt saying 'it's the better plane' . . . there was even a story of three scruffy airmen 'skiving off' in duty hours to an out-of-bounds pub beyond the outer marker, there joined by a polite man in neat civilian clothes who had enquired amicably what they were doing 'this far from home'.

"Said to be an AOC's inspection," rejoined Fitter LAC Burroughs, more generally known as 'Letch'.

"Funny, that I should know nothing about that. You see, I'm the AOC." Doubt had been cast upon this tale, but it was agreed to be in character.

John was often reminded of the nervous little man in Dickens, with the straight-backed military wife, saying, 'Discipline must be Maintained.' This task devolved mostly upon Corporal Phillips, i.c. Abbalutions, fond of saying, 'I peg you, mate,' when putting them on a charge, so that there might be people on jankers, an occasion for Lenny to become Corporal Buttonstick and show zeal.

John remained as unseen as was humanly possible; jankers-wallahs (odd, how much of the old 'India' vocabulary

persisted: char, and a shufti at the bints) were supposed to be
paraded by Len and inspected by the Orderly Officer – not
when this was him.

In all circumstances he kept very quiet about the Secret.
One should remember that he was only twenty in 1947.
Robert, his father, had married a German woman. He was
Magda's son also . . .

This state of affairs had not lasted long. It was agreed
among the family, shocked about 'the Boche woman' that
this was an eccentricity of Robert's or perhaps a moment-
of-weakness. The child knew very little about it. Things
had been hushed up; matters had been arranged, lawyers
called into play. Later, at boarding school, one never
spoke in any case of family. The boy was sensitive, knew
perhaps better than to be curious. By 1939 the German
woman had been obliterated for eight years; the boy
barely knew who his mother had been, not at all what had
become of her: very vaguely, that she'd 'gone back where
she belonged'. During the war, and by then the less said or
thought the better, Robert had himself died: there were,
scarce seen, trustees. Truthfully, John had never thought
about it at all seriously. Finding himself now an English
boy, and under orders – one really did not think of oneself
as holding the King's Commission; one was just another
dogsbody, shovelled off like hundreds more to do a thor-
oughly unwanted stint in the Occupation Forces, and what
was the point of that? This fucking war is now supposed to
be over. We're getting told a lot of crap about the
Russians. John had been sent here, instead of to Istres
(down somewhere near Marseille) or that stinking Canal
Zone (permanganate in the vegetables; Wogs and
Fucking-Fayid) and really one knew nothing about
Germans. What senior officers thought and said – but
they had a right to say what they pleased; they had fought

this people and felt respect for it and they did not talk about 'Boches'.

But now – one was beginning to find out. One is 'half-boche', but it doesn't show and nobody knows about it, and one isn't going to mention it, either.

Dogsbody John got dogsbody chores. These were never clearly defined; Flight-Lieutenant Marshall was utterly uninterested. John's days were spent picking up dropped stitches; motor-transport one moment, censorship the next: nothing was explained and he had to learn never to complain. One wasn't here to do or die but merely to be shat upon. Medically downgraded, too – boy, you could be fucked about much worse, and the essential is to be on good, flexible, humble terms with Flight-Sergeant Lafferty, who holds your weekend pass, the 36, the 48, in the hollow of his hand, not to speak of leave and maybe a place in a plane that will be landing on Hornchurch this afternoon – even squadron-leaders grovelled for that one.

These duties had quite often much to do with Germans. If, unofficially, Germans are there to be shat on or concil-iated as the case might be, the official line was to be polite, co-operative, paternal, even rather kindly. Nato began to be talked about, and in broadminded circles the notion began even to be adumbrated that eventually one might find oneself welcoming uh, a bulwark, a sort of buffer, against the dread Bolshies: Transport Command is said to be taking Berlin very seriously. The talk about air-lifting did not much affect these potty little units in the Rhineland, but the name of Adenauer was trickling down. Hereabouts they were Catholic, y'know, not ever very nazi, and getting the Germans back into the way of municipal administra-tion is a Good Thing.

So that meeting Gunther was a great help: here was a thread-of-Ariadne, all right.

He was in the little office he shared with Mr Marshall; shared, that is, when Mr Marshall whose assistant he was termed was there, which wasn't often. Lafferty came strolling in; he never knocked or anything; hands in his pockets as usual.

"Mr Charles. Top of the morning to you." If he ever did say Sir it sounded like an insult. "I've a Brownie on the telephone, not Brigade I fancy." Air Force word for the Army, in exchange for 'Blueboys'. "Asking for your kind master, would you like to take that?"

"Have it put through here if you would, Flight Sergeant." Clearing his throat, to get his voice deeper. "Admin here, P/O Charles. Mr Marshall's away just now."

"Good Morning." A high voice, not though a twitter. "Maitland at Traffic Control. It's about that bridge at Wicked."

"Yes, I know about it. Been marked unsafe for ages." Our way of saying Wickede; the village of Neheim was always known as Knee-high, but that could be said of almost anywhere.

"Well, I've been on at Group for ages. You're really more concerned than we are."

"Everybody complains about having to make the détour." Tactful.

"I told your sergeant –"

"Not mine, thank God," hoping Lafferty was listening.

"Thing is, Brigade tells me that the REs have agreed to fix it. But as you know the Germans – yes, quite. I was thinking, there's a German fellow who is helpful in this sort of affair. It's a Mr Mahback, and he's to be found over your way, I thought it might be tactful if you had a word, donchaknow."

"Obliged to you, Mr Maitland, and wilco. I'll lay that on."

"Okay old chap, roger and thank you."

Herr Marbach was indeed to be found, and rarity, where he said, in a patched-up office where paperwork and rubber stamps were beginning to function. Thumb-tacks in evidence, with a lot of German Nomenclature of that complex structure John could make little of; what did 'Standesamt' mean? 'Secrétaire à la Mairie' probably covered it, but the man had a broad honest face, a good smile, and spoke a slow but clear and grammatical English: plainly a man of education as well as the intelligence and character hinted at.

"Please don't get up. That's a good fire you have there and I'm glad to see it." A stove rigged, and a pile of sawed pine logs; half-dry, but with the damper open . . . "Charles," holding his hand out. One had learned that the Germans waited for one to do this.

In quite a few days he came to rely upon Mr Marbach for a remarkably varied number of the knotty little whatnots. John had also learned a good deal about him. And at his request was calling him Gunther. It was something like a friendship, without familiarity or condescension. I was a silly young boy, timid and awkward, standing-on-my-dignity when I didn't know what to do, which was nearly always. We had little enough to do with Squadron, which was twenty miles off and the whole point of the 'satellite' was that we got the chores they didn't want to be bothered with. They had a flying-field; runways and hangars, a tower, planes to repair and maintain. If I did have occasion to go over there (which was seldom) I acquired some slight reputation for 'getting on well with the Huns'. 'Tail-end Charlie knows a bod.' Gunther was my secret weapon. His thorough knowledge of municipal administration, of what were the beginnings of local government, his experience with bureaucracy, his knowing everyone in the region –

and he was always patient, a quiet listener, just paternal enough. He did it well. No doubt my ignorance and naiveté served him, too. I gained in confidence. I even became fairly competent at my work. It was his suggestion that I should learn German.

Less than a year later John had become 'the local authority' on all things German. Things had changed. Only a week before – "Nobody ever gets posted out of a dump like this," said F/O Bridgman resentfully. "I've done everything but kiss Lafferty's behind." And now he was gone, and Lafferty too. And even Joe, his devious and complex system of peculation impenetrable to the last. The 'old men' were long gone: there were few survivors among the veterans. Sergeant Smyth still played the piano in pubs for the 'demob parties' when the good-old-days were drunkenly yearned over, and the old songs brimmed with sentiment.

> *Oh Salome, Oh you should See Salome*
> *Standing there, with her tits all bare*
> *Every little wiggle makes the boys all stare . . .*

Among the airmen there was a new intake of Spikes and Tinys and Loftys, if scarcely less casual and travel-stained than the old lot. The black market was not what it was. It took now a whole carton of Chesterfields, and only a fraction of the effect upon Foe and Fräulein. And now there were rumours that the entire unit would shortly be disbanded. The Army, the Air Force, the Control Commission had come belatedly to the conclusion that there was little point in keeping guard upon former Luftwaffe airfields; not to speak of the quantities of 'stores' which so unaccountably vanished. There was a rumour, even, that an entire fighter plane, obsolete perhaps but in working order, had been left parked 'out on the perimeter' in the old dispersal style, and had disappeared by morning leaving only an oilstain on the grass. 'Last master stroke by Joe,' said the cognoscenti; 'flogged to the Arabs.'

John, by now himself looking forward to being demobbed some day (no sign of a posting; perhaps he had made himself too useful – the Adj was tight-lipped about losing him), had a new worry. Barbara was pregnant and it was beginning to show. As Fräuleins went she had been a considerable feather in his cap, being seventeen, a ripe-corn blonde and very pretty; as everybody agreed, 'a smashing pair of tits'. (I can smell her hair now. Cheap shampoo. 'Drene' would it have been? Or 'Friday night's Amami night'? Babes in the wood, the two of them; myself as innocent as her.) Most enterprising airmen had local milkmaids. The more sophisticated preferred older, married women. On the satellite there was no Naafi or 'supplies', but Sergeant Pratt (well-named) had a cosy little corner shop with useful things like stockings and lipstick. Barbara was well brought up, of a respectable family (without a father, like many more); clearly 'an officer's piece', being shy, withdrawn, nice-mannered, and impeccably clean . . . All the easier, to work one's evil will upon. The summer of 1947 was hot, dry, propitious to hayfield romance, and John was lavish with bribes to the M/T section. Access once gained to those smashing tits . . . John went on leave to Paris, and came back with goodies. Stockings of course were treasures. I remember a Lucien Lelong perfume, and earrings, and tortoiseshell combs for her hair. I remember lengths of cotton material which made up into summer frocks. And I remember her mother, a thin, still good-looking woman with harried eyes. Talking my stilted, halting German. A kind, quiet woman, pointing her eyes elsewhere . . . I brought her food, of course. Sugar, flour, cheese. Soap. Needles and thread.

Barbara did not whore for goodies. She was a virgin, and she had self-respect, and she worried long, anxiously, about virtue. The lecherous soldiery did not gain mastery with any ease: the surrender when it came was dramatic, and there were tears. But from there on – so yes, I remember, and with joy and without really much vanity: a twilit Barbara stark naked running in a hayfield: at night a naked boy and girl in a river. The Ruhr is not much of a river. Upon occasion it is deep enough and wide enough to swim in. I remember owls. I am (I should bloody well hope so) sensitive to smells. A meticulously-scrubbed seventeen-year-old girl in the Ruhrland: she did not smell of stale flesh, of urine or cheap make-up. In those years there were no chemical deodorants. Barbara smelt of hay and clean girl, and of love, faith, and loyalty. No, I am not sentimentalising. And if she had a period she didn't think of sucking me off, and I would never have thought of asking it of her.

So that when she said she'd missed a period, and then two, I wasn't going to talk about this to any Medical Officer. (The Early-Treatment hut, generally found just inboard of camp guardrooms. The Free From Infection inspections. One could easily feel that the obsession with venereal disease set narrow limits to Army medicine.) Preferable, decidedly, to bring a problem to Gunther. Something of a habit by then. He listened, which few people do.

Is it all sufficiently clear? I mean his position, situation, as well as character. Dr Adenauer was building his Federal Republic upon people like this, as much as upon the Trümmerfrauen, those amazing women who cleared rubble in the early days by hand.

"Let me think about this overnight, would you?"

Gunther would have been forty, or just over; deep-chested, bull-necked, pale brown hair beginning to slip back off a fine forehead. The family was solidly implanted for several generations, Rhinelanders with a strong sense of religion and of Heimat. The elder brother was a farmer who had been prosperous, and would be so again, generous to his land, good to his animals. Not notables, but respected well-regarded people, straight dealers who gave their word seldom and kept it. Gunther lived in the town, in a bombed house which he was rebuilding in his spare time, which he always seemed to find. He had never sought an official position under the National Socialist régime, which he detested, but his natural talent for administration meant prominence in most local affairs; fire brigade or hospital; sewers or the water supply.

He was fairly taciturn about all this. John asked one day where he had learned his English (he was interested in languages, and took pains to widen his vocabulary, but had not been to the University). No, but he'd had a wife who had English connections. Not very forthcoming: oh, she had died, in the bombing. One did not pursue the subject. He allowed himself some impersonal interest of a similar sort.

"And you, Mr Charles? When your time here is up? The University, will it be?"

"I suppose so," vaguely. One was still in a time when it seemed one would never get out of the Army; a temporary Lieutenant meaning 'placeholder' for ever and ever. The joke went down well; Gunther was interested in names.

"Charles, is that a common name? Not like Smith and Miller."

"Oh, I don't know. Commonplace, at least; I've never thought about it. Like Thomson or Jackson. Ordinary."

He lived by himself; one child, a daughter, little girl of fourteen or so, shy and well-mannered, lived with him: one saw her sometimes 'doing her homework'. Name of Sibylle; this also a 'commonplace' name hereabouts. In

English Sybil, funny how the vowels had got transposed, but the English couldn't spell.

"Mr Pepys – he was a civil servant in the seventeenth century, wrote a diary; man who would interest you – spells the same name four or five different ways. Shakespeare did the same, including his own. Why is there nobody called Shakesword, one wonders. Chap called Armour was with me at school." Quite the little literary gent, already, our John.

"I've been thinking about Barbara," when Gunther was next seen. "A nice girl; I know her well, and her family – her father was a good man. I don't want any nonsense of old women muttering there goes another one up-to-no-good. I wouldn't want to see her visiting the angel-makers either. I don't mind saying to you, since I've got to know you quite well, that this is no matter for you, or the military authority either. The holy nuns? I wouldn't feel keen at all about that. Putting the baby out for adoption – possible but at best a poor solution. I've talked to her, she wants to keep it." Abruptly. "I'll marry her myself if she'll have me." John was dumbfounded but had the sense to stay so.

John never heard the end of it because his posting came through quite soon. Back to England, to a dreary East Anglian station. That clerk at Innsworth again, shaping destinies. But six months more and the 'temporary place-holder' was demobbed and reading English at Cambridge, with other things than Germans to think about.

If he thought about it at all, it was with gratitude. To Germany because there he had got rid of the idiotic pre-judices still obtaining and all too frequent, as well as a few of his more personal hangups. And to the Air Force too, which had changed again and fundamentally, into something highly serious and professional, so that the interval of nobody knowing or caring could now be seen as richly comic – even a valuable furtherance of one's education: without this he would have got nothing out of university.

John woke 'feeling quite well'. No headache, and rested, like a man who had slept well. Time to take stock of the surroundings, as well as to mobilise, to get a grip upon himself, to be ready; if need be, to defend, where possible. Knowing nothing, understanding nothing, it was hard to know what to be ready for. It looked uncommonly like imprisonment. They weren't then – who were 'they'? – thinking of simply hitting him on the head out of a dark corner. There was planning here, and preparation. Was he kidnapped for ransom? Was the idea to hold him in secret for any length of time? Was he going to be put on trial by some crackpot revolutionary committee? Germany is full of crackpots, but why him? Where was he, anyhow? He had been heavily – beuh, it had been horrible – anaesthetised: they could well have brought him a considerable way, in the back of that car. Had it even to do with the odd and uncomfortable occurrences of these last weeks? That, anyhow, one had to believe.

Daylight called for a detective. What can one deduce? For a start, he'd been living out of suitcases, these were on the floor – they'd got his car. This produced an abrupt clutch of fear. Nobody would look for him because nobody would know where to start. Even if Cathy remembered which airport (and why should she?) and even if two bored policemen remembered that an odd-looking man had said he was going to Arnsburg – there was nothing to show he'd ever been near the place, and now he could be anywhere. It would furthermore be several weeks before anyone thought of asking . . .

If, this minute, he floated out of the skylight on a magic carpet – it stands hygienically open and he listened. There were no street noises; ergo he was not in a town. No handy cow or chicken noises to tell him this was country. The likeliest place would be some quiet residential suburb, where people do not take that keenly-burning interest in their neighbours' movements that he'd be pleased to know about.

What could one tell from the house? That it too was silent; ergo solidly constructed and it had the feeling of size. Some ugly but massive, comfortable villa, perhaps in its own grounds. Since part of the roof sloped he was in an attic. Panelled top and sides in pitchpine, for insulation. Not very recent since there were unfaded areas where pictures had been taken off the walls. Furniture built in to the slope; clothes cupboard, chest of drawers, table-top desk, all empty. Brass handles to give a 'cabin' impression; a boy's room and he thought of the 'two young men'. A door at the back led to a simple bathroom, shower unit, washbasin and lavatory. Another door behind, locked, gave one to believe there would be another bedroom. The skylights showed sky; not very helpful. The floor was plain carpeting with a springy underlay; the boards below would be uneven. The door had been drilled for a 'judas' spyglass; they had prepared then, for his coming? No wicket or shelf for food; they weren't afraid of his breaking out or making an outcry. It increased the helpless feel.

As though on cue steps sounded, heavy but dulled as though by matting. Bolts were drawn. A 'young man' blank-faced, unspeaking, scarcely looking at him, appearing uninterested. A metal tray with a teashop coffee-pot that holds two cups. Pub sugar-lumps and the little plastic pot of evap. milk; the same of jam. Bread and a slice of sausage. Plate, cup, saucer, plastic knife and spoon. Prison fare but a modern, humane sort of prison. The young man went out as he came and John drank the coffee gratefully:

it was hot, strong, and of good quality. The bread was German, neither good nor bad. At the sound of a far-off plane he went to look – there, a tiny silver toy, bright in the sunlight. He remembered a tale from the thirties, of a man imprisoned who had noticed a plane passing every night at the same hour and got a message out: his friends found him by this means. John smiled at this prewar innocence.

The momentary lift of hot fresh coffee passed and depression gained on him. Ranged along the bathroom wall had been an exercise bike. They meant to keep him then, and not to let him out. There was no book or newspaper, not even a pocket chess set. On the desk top lay his notebook and his two pens. Perhaps they meant him to write a book. 'Well-known writer Retires to Hermitage, to compose his Memoirs.' One could always ask for things. The young man had not looked forthcoming. Nobody John could ever recall seeing. That glimpse yesterday – was it even yesterday? – didn't count, and his companion, the driver . . . presumably they'd take turns with the jailer's chores. The plate and cup were ordinary pub china. One could break that stuff; use it as a weapon? They weren't afraid; what would he do – cut his own wrists? A big young man, strong-boned, tanned, an athletic look.

Feeling of helplessness – what the hell did they want, or expect of him? He put the tray on the floor by the door: why should he be disturbed more than he must? Straighten, tidy, make the bed; one must maintain self-respect. Go shave, brush your teeth. Shave . . . they'd thought of that; a little battery machine, the sort one charged by plugging it in to a socket. Given a blade, even poor old Charles might be thought dangerous. He lay down on the bed – a thing forbidden in prisons during the daytime. He closed his eyes; he had thinking to do.

He fell in fact into a light doze, which since he had slept

long meant only that he was in a dozy frame of mind: if
there'd been any drug it was out of his system. Or had they
put bromide in the coffee – that ineradicable conviction of
all English soldiers! He lay there, not functioning at all, the
mind as limp and spineless as the limbs. He didn't hear
footsteps this time. The bolts were drawn gently as though
unwilling to frighten or disturb him. The door opened; he
rolled his head lazily and opened one eye; a languid movement with the smallest dash of curiosity, like a lemon slice
in a glass of water.

A woman stood in the doorway looking at him. Still, not
speaking. He blinked; it was as though his eyelids were
paralysed. So were the muscles of his throat, his arm and
hand – all of him. But unmistakably – a phantom? The
brain, slow, lame, sent a soggy image, blurred like a television screen when someone has turned on a circular
saw – he could hear the saw, screaming in his ear as it bit
in to wood, the wood of his stupid skull. That, there, was
Sibylle.

They remained so, immobile both, for a minute or
more: it was as though neither could quite trust their eyes.
The attic passage behind her was dimly lit and the shad-
owed figure in the doorway seemed shrouded, spectre-like.
Did she take a step forward? A clear steel-grey daylight was
filling the room, lighting her features from above: his
thought was 'she is quite unchanged'. Thinner, greyer,
older as was natural; the face seemed no more lined that
when . . . This stillness, that gravity was familiar; so as a
young woman just married, 'acquiring experience', she
stood in front of a shop, before a market stall, considering.
'Studying' – a characteristic word of hers; she did not slap-
dash at things like him. Only in part was it the habit of a
frugal childhood, the economical housewife turning sous
round in her pocket. So would she look at a picture he had

bought, for long days, before deciding whether she wanted to live with it.

He had easily become irritable. Taste, imagination, the 'coup d'oeil'; this she had not. In a theatre, he might be taken with the dash, the technical attack of an actress – 'her sexual attractions have nothing to do with it'. It might be only next day that she let fall 'meretricious'. Alert on the instant to the cry or movement of a restless child, at any moment of the night. He might feel the forehead, say 'feverish'; she would know, and decide. In England they promote their pleaders, their barristers, to judgeships, and one may suppose there are worse methods. Sibylle had no oratorical gift, nor skill with written word (her letters, in his absences, were conventionally plodding). But she would have made an exceptional judge. About a human being, butcher or publisher, painter or plumber, he had never known her wrong. It was as though her only real mistake had been himself.

Asking to marry her – impulse, instinct? Gunther, formally consulted 'for the girl's hand' had said little. 'She's young, but she's good at making up her own mind.' Certainly no young girl dazzled by any 'Backfisch' romanticism. She had 'chosen'.

Men never seem to understand anything. Men say, 'Damned women. Menopause.' Really he had done no better. Sexually she remained intensely exciting, into middle age and beyond. I am not going into any vulgar details: one stirred the witches' pot and alchemies resulted. One never felt that one had more than scratched, superficially. Writers; listening to themselves talk! 'Are you looking at yourself in the glass?' she would ask. She had judged him, found him not good enough.

Terribly sorry; smallest possible word about adulteries, here. She never 'envisaged'. German peasant girl, put a wedding ring on and you won't get it off, not in the tomb. Simply never entered her head. He . . .? Sure, the not-seeing what one does not intend to see. It all got written on the slate. In uncanny detail; one would be sure she'd been standing there in the room . . . She loved thee, cruel Moor. Harsh line that; amongst others, harsher still.

A funny thing – leastways I hope that it's funny – that I can look at a Hamlet or a Macbeth with the detachment of a glacier: this one never fails to wring my bowels.

I am hit by Othello's 'technical' remark of, 'I have another sword within this chamber'; as though the man had just broken his pen; the way I'd talk of a ballpoint run dry. I think of little Albertine Sarrazin in prison saying, My Bic, that's my pistol. Any writer will understand what I mean. Myself, all my adulteries were literary.

Once, a child was taken to the Verdi opera. Suddenly it jumped up and screamed. 'Stop. Stop.' Kleiber stopped instantly and turned. The child said, 'Can't you see that he's going to kill her?' He signalled to Desdemona, who got up, came forward and made her very grandest curtsey, the two men their deepest bow, and the whole house applauded the astounded child. It was not I, alas.

In our house people didn't kill each other, we only wrote about it. And one fine day Sibylle threw a few things into a little bag and walked out of the door without saying a word. Didn't curtsey, neither. She didn't believe in killing people. Being German she tended to say there'd been enough killing.

Kleiber held the orchestra in a moment of concentrated silence, started it from the exact note he'd left off, the child's father and mother held it between them, deeply ashamed, and yet proud. So must Verdi have been proud.

Later on, as he supposed around midday, there was a midday meal. This was a curried beef stew, which came with a rather sour orange, which he didn't eat, and a banana which he kept in case of feeling hungry later. When evening came the supper dish was again a good vegetable soup, and two pieces of bread and butter. Yes; in jail the food becomes important. It marks the passage of time. It relieves monotony. A human being brings it, even if he doesn't speak.

He did a good few kilometres too, one way or another, on the exercise bike. Those at least he could count, since the thing had a meter. One looks forward, childishly, to getting the same figure six times in a row. One sympathises with those, in America or elsewhere, who suffer from the 'indeterminate sentence'. Not knowing what one has to serve, nor, very frequently, why, is no doubt of it a cruelty. He thought of the last time he had been in jail, which was some years ago. He looked through the notebook, wondering if anything there might shed light on present circumstances – it didn't.

But he had one certainty, now. The moment, that morning, had not been a hallucination. It had really been Sibylle standing there. He could feel sure, silly as it sounds, on account of the curry. A dish that he is Britishly fond of, and which isn't really native to Germany. It had been 'his' fantasy, and he had taught it to Sibylle in days long gone, to put dried apricots in the stew. They might do that in Silesia with pork, but not in the Rheinland. She had been a careful, reliable, but unimaginative cook. Respectful of his caprices. It was like her somehow to acquire the habit without quite knowing where it came from. Or was it perhaps some sort of message: would there be others?

One had no means of knowing whether they did put some sedative in some dish of this sort. Hide the taste, maybe? These things come in pretty colours. Shiny coating, gelatine, slips down easy and one doesn't think about the inside. Vile, very likely. Because I fell into a deep sleep. What was there to do but go to bed early? And dreamed; vividly, unpleasantly.

Now then, John, you are a writer of experience. Know better than to give any value to dreams. They may seem striking at the time but are worthless in fiction. Occasionally he has tried them out, on psycho-analyst friends. The interpretations can be entertaining, not much better. As Marie Lloyd put it, after eating lobster, 'The great big Albert Hall had turned into a pub . . .' Writing it all down is just another example of writers' neurosis.

Nothing else to do. Awake now, miasma of nightmare still heavy but awake, amenable to reason. Neurotic since all time. Paranoia, schizophrenia, blah blah, it's only psychotic if you're crippled by it.

Look, this is simple, John, you are seventy years old, the prostate not what it was. Made irritable, probably by sitting on the hard saddle of that damned exercise bike. So you get up and pee. One is reminded of Mr Pepys; in a strange house, afflicted by a looseness in the night, and damn that chambermaid who has forgotten the pot. He had a shit 'in the chimney' – and what's more he wrote it all down. And so will I.

The air from the skylight is fresh, countrified, silent. Trees somewhere near, eating carbon dioxide, pouring out oxygen. I switch on the light, to write.

There was a cow, delightful cow, of a specific French breed, most attractive. Can't now call the name to mind, neither a Blonde d'Aquitaine nor a Montbéliarde; cherish these local breeds, they're like long-forgotten kinds of apple. Small cows, agile, intelligent, nothing like great dimwit milk-factory Friesians. Good-looking too; the local farmers swear by them, grow much attached to these charming beasts.

Hm, the more backward peasant will fuck absolutely anything; John is unfamiliar with such habits. Never mind; this cow is in fact a woman. A witch, to be sure; shape-changing is one of the surest methods of recognising them.

Standing in a field of spring grass, outrageously green and full of buttercups. Facing diagonally away, in a dancer's elegant and complicated stance, the head turned to look at him along her shoulder. Wide liquid eyes, curious and expectant, and the tail switching slowly. There is a rich, rustic, clovery smell. One would give, in passing, a comfortable affectionate slap upon this silky quivery flank. The robe, as the French call the coat, of this kind of cow is also a well-known attractive feature.

At that exact moment she turned into a woman and burst into laughter. The dancer's pose was unchanged. The woman was naked. John could put a name to this cow. So could Sibylle.

Of no interest, so far. Conceivably a short story, something after the manner of my old mate Pat Highsmith who rather specialised in such, but the scene changed abruptly.

An apartment in an old house, in Paris. Comfortable if rather dark, and with lots of wasted space. Their bedroom opened on a passage, ill-ventilated, with carpeting which smelt, much complained of by Sibylle, a keen scrubwoman who tracked French dirt.

The perplexing feature was that he kept coming out of this bedroom and finding himself, instead of the familiar smelly corridor, in a secret passage. A door opened and one was in the witch's lair. Décor by Gustav Klimt, and a strong scent of Schiaparelli.

This wouldn't do at all. Witches invading one's living quarters, that's much too blatant.

He killed the cow, of course. Big long knife like an old-fashioned bayonet, he drove it in behind the shoulder. He had no wish to cause her pain but she looked at him with hurt and perplexity in those lovely violet eyes, sinking slowly to her knees, lying there still elegant in death. Between the witch in the field and the little cow in the lair, smelling now strongly of blood, there was a gap, but dreams are like that, worthless for even trivial railway-journey fiction.

Undoubtedly the witch was Hungarian. He thought of Daffodil; very nice too; sometimes one only wishes to sprawl lollingly upon Klimt-decorative cushions; eat chocolates while having one's toenails painted. Not Daffodil. Much brighter and more terrifying, the old joke about them going in to the revolving door behind one and coming out in front . . . Fast talkers, spot-the-lady men (like Kollo). Like the two sisters, young girls, championship chess players, one can feel sure that all their opponents will be quite convinced they are witches.

The dream finished in a scene brilliantly lit, making love upon an immense leather sofa, in some place of colossal gloom and grandeur, like the Travellers' Club, there were fascinated onlookers and she said quite indignantly, 'What do you take me for, an exhibitionist?' Her name was Ilona, she had silver hair.

No no no, her name was Albertina, she lived in Paris, she had tawny hair, lioness looks, she was Austrian or maybe South German, some confusion existed about that and most likely deliberate.

The trouble here was that Paris was not big enough a town to hold two women together.

One thought, as one quite often did, about Mr Pepys.

Attacked on all sides. Courtiers, parliamentarians, crooked contractors, every bribing bastard seeking to get a finger in the pie, his own colleagues praising him while planting knives, the King worse than useless ('Give him a whore and a shoulder of mutton,' said Oliver, 'and he'll always be happy'). He's worried out of his mind, hardly sleeps, and he's losing his sight. Trying to read through paper tubes; the Royal Society doesn't understand much yet about optical lenses. The English are humiliated and furious at having their arse kicked rotten by the Dutch, in war at sea, and he is trying to concoct a defence, dictating it to his clerks when he can't see to write.

His wife is a sweet woman, true, good, honest. She complains a lot, of isolation, neglect, the hungry boredom of having nothing useful to do. He loves her dearly, arranges for occupations, instrumental music and singing lessons, buys books for her to read to him, is generous with clothes and jewellery, parties, outings, and endless visits to the theatre. These are the delights he most enjoys – but so does she.

Will one be surprised that he's sneaking off pretty often after the girls? He has two or three rather shopworn mistresses, but there are barmaids, actresses, and a number of respectable bourgeois wives, unaverse to having their tits fiddled with, skirts lifted, treating him to a wank in the back of the coach. He writes it all down, the sexy bits in a ludicrous kitchen Spanish; what would my psychiatrist make of that?

Deb is Elizabeth's companion more than maid, sharing in treats and outings; a nice young girl, pretty and innocent. He likes her to comb his hair; it quietens his nerves, and so does sliding his hand up her skirt. One morning Elizabeth crashes in on them, and there is the devil to pay.

There are few pages, I think, in which naked suffering is so baldly set down. 'Poor wretch,' he says, of both women. He realises that he loves both, and is in hideous torment. He is too honest to say it of himself.

Elizabeth's pain is the more fearful to see. She is his faithful wife; she has resisted temptations. She exacts a hideous revenge and one bleeds for the three of them. How Stendhal, that other fumbling, incompetent lover, mopping blood from his own written pages, would have loved to know Pepys, and go out drinking with him.

We, literary buggers, are like doctors. People suffer, it would be unbearable, had we not as students learned the techniques of blocking emotion. Policemen, social assistants, the Salvation Army, all must learn the same basic truth.

This dawdling, John, in front of an open window, won't do. Wisdom points to getting back into bed, stretching out. Breathe evenly, unwind; one does sleep, eventually.

Thus the second day of imprisonment began with oversleeping. He heard no footsteps, no bolts; nobody shouted wakey-wakey. There was a sensation that somebody was in the room; there was a smell of coffee. Sibylle stood there, looking up at a grey rainy sky. He got out with a jump, but grainy and lethargic; vulnerable.

"Put your dressing-gown on, dear, it's chilly." Housewifely closing the skylight, turning the radiator up. It was disproportionally irritating to be called 'dear'.

"Thanks, I'm going to have a shower," in a gruff, cross voice like a child being disobedient in an effort to show independence.

"Drink your coffee first or it'll be cold." Which was unanswerable. There was only one chair. She remained standing, looking out as though wondering how long the rain was going to last. "Give me your dirty things and I'll get them washed." Her trousers and shirt were as in the 'vision' of the day before: had she been wearing a cardigan or was it chillier this morning? It would be better to adopt the housewifely, practical tone, much as though these eight years had telescoped into the one day. So that he sat down, poured himself coffee, stirred it, didn't want to eat, did want overwhelmingly a cigarette.

"Sibylle, I seem to be out of fags, can you find me some?"

"No." The voice was not sharp, but the monosyllable still had the effect of a slap.

"So." Controlling his voice into this impersonal level compass. "Are you proposing to have me killed?" She turned around to face him then, and said, "Good heavens, no. I want to make you alive."

The coffee was lukewarm, muddy.

"Then you owe me some explanations, don't you? I've had several – I don't know what to call them – apparently accidental close shaves, which have now come to appear deliberately engineered, from . . . from, I dislike this word it has such a melodramatic sound, but assassination. My house was burned down. Now I find myself kidnapped by two young ruffians. I have to suppose you are answerable for all this, that it has somehow been planned or directed by you. If the idea was to give me a big shock or fright it certainly succeeds. Not at all like you, I should have thought. Whatever I suspected or imagined, it . . . it never entered my head.

"You, you of all people, forever going on about morals and ethics, it certainly does all take my breath away. Starting from zero I should like to hear what all this is about."

"I suppose some things do need explaining. It wasn't rehearsed. It wasn't all neatly plotted, like in a book. Perhaps that is the way it started. That you should find yourself inside one of your own books. But even there – they sometimes take unexpected turns, don't they?

"But now you've seen me" . . . She went on, "I don't

want all these explanations, they're no good, are they? Like the last page of an old-fashioned detective story. You always used to say one mustn't explain, it had to be self-explanatory but one had to think about it. That's what you have to do, that's what you're here for, we're going to give you the time you need."

"Need need, feed, bleed, what is this nonsense? Who are 'We'? Where are we, whose house is this? Is this Gunther's house, has he something to do with this?"

"This is my house, dear. Gunther is dead. He was old, you know. You'll understand. It took me some time to understand. But I am stupid, as you always told me, and you are a very intelligent man and you've lived a long time and had a great deal of experience. So you will understand. It's high time you did. It's bound to be a little bit painful at first. Like the cigarettes. Or your house. These are all things you can perfectly well do without."

"Sibylle, I quite often used to think you were a wee bit mad. Not that it mattered; so am I, so are we all. But this you know is not just illegal, nobody cares much about that. Or immoral and unethical – good heavens, you know, this is quite insane, pathologically so."

"Go and have your shower, that'll be a good start. I do have to explain things though. You spoke about two young ruffians who brutalised you. Start thinking now about this, while you shave and so on. Those two boys whom you describe as ruffians are your grandchildren. There's something for you to go to work upon," with the first little flick she had shown of spitefulness. Was it? Or sarcasm? One didn't argue, with Sibylle. Never mind the years intervening, there nothing had changed; years and years ago one learned that with a woman 'argument', what in male company one thinks of as a discussion based upon more or less logical lines (we may disagree; he has his logic, as I have mine, we may be starting from totally opposed stand-points), is impossible. Their minds do not work as ours do. They have also a hideous skill at acquiring and making use of our own phrases. One breaks off the engagement, before it turns into a sort of judo contest, taking care not to slam the bathroom door.

What on earth? (One had to get used to the little ways of this shower: hot water took a while to arrive, and the mixer tap was not very clever either: one had to add the cold drop by drop or it would suddenly go much too cold, dis-agreeably.) Then, having to use an electric shaver; somehow one's beard grew the wrong way. It would have to be trained, because one went over the same patch and it still didn't feel properly clean.

Sibylle was gone, taking the cold coffee with her. One would now just love a properly hot cup of coffee, and one could just go on loving. Part of the 'plan' – whatever that was – appeared to include depriving him of alcohol and of tobacco. Extremely unwelcome since John is heavily dependent upon both. But that can be managed; he was perfectly aware that these deprivations, however unpleas-ant, would only do him good. As French prime ministers are fond of saying, there is no government without constraint.

She was looking very healthy. Let's see – he had to do some sums, anyway, and this was a good place to start (John always vague about dates). Knows at least his own age, and that she is five years younger. He had several times forgot-ten her birthday, a source of much and not necessarily hidden grievance: the times he remembered to buy a good present, and arrive triumphant with flowers at breakfast-time, only made the other occasions worse; she had the memory usually ascribed to elephants. (Why Elephants? Has this ever been satisfactorily demonstrated?) She liked to eat and drink, and a talent had been to stop, apparently at will; that was a trim figure, a clear complexion; women half her age would envy both. And in trousers, which really suit very few women, one noticed first the unusual length of thigh, a narrow waist and that marvellous slim behind. John surprised himself considerably by feeling a sharp uprush of desire.

And hell, why not? She is my wife. We've never actually been divorced. Come to that, and knowing her, she has very probably never been to bed with another man.

But to business, and small addition-subtraction sums in the notebook. The year of their marriage, the child had been a boy (nice little boy) of four. Barbara twenty-two, married, by the look of things very happily married. Gunther would have been fifty or a scrap over. Unimportant; he neither looked it nor (he said) felt it. One scarcely noticed the gap between them, anyhow a commonplace in a second marriage (and his first wife, dead under bombing in 'forty-two or -three – that whole miserable time had been left behind, cut cleanly away).

Wasn't that the year also of the great English disillusion? The loss of confidence? It went much deeper than the perpetual nagging grumble with which Robert's beastly relatives conducted their lives (inflicted daily upon himself). 'Who Won the War? Jerries!' England so pale and shabby, with even then uncleared bombsites, and rationing barely over. They had never got over the surrender of Singapore and the patronising, kindly can-do of Our American Allies. Why, even disgraced, humbled, tatty France was so much more fun, and so much more energetic too, in those early 'fifties – even before the General came back, the poor silly Fourth Republic had set many a project afoot afterwards claimed by Gaullists. Nowadays of course historians would put the decline of the Empire much further back. Even the Diamond Jubilee had been full of cracks, and as for the Scramble for Africa . . . Wasn't the downfall due to the total refusal to see or accept? They went on to this day singing about the Land of Hope and Glory, and everything that went wrong was the fault of the Jerries, the General, and the Upstarts.

Whereas here it was the time of Professor Erhard's Miracle, and not a ruin in sight. You could walk down the Königsallee in Dusseldorf and come still to open space, but levelled and grass-grown, just waiting for Allianz and Basf and Siemens. English officers still swaggered about (he could recognise them in the street, each with the face that had been his only five years ago). There was still a Control Commission, or whatever they called it now, and BAOR; soldiers getting drunk (in, say, Minden) after a football match.

What had brought him back? What complex bundle of psychological threads now pulled – he had thought it the lost, obliterated German mother driven out with the hatred and derision so many in England still feel and show and mouth. It was a lot more than that.

But one wasn't going to brood about all that now, today. Simple friendship towards Gunther, that straight, honest, just man. A kindness, and goodwill, towards Barbara, a good and generous girl. He had wanted to see them, wanted to know them happy. A bit of vanity, also: he had written and published his first books, and they existed now in German translation, and the 'official' reason for his voyage was to talk business in Hamburg – one wasn't averse to a display of newfound confidence and even splendour.

What a welcome they'd given him. Simple, utterly unaffected. Glad to see him? He'd 'dropped in' and they insisted he stay, and on his way back from Hamburg he'd stayed again, a fortnight, and when he left he took Sibylle with him. 'Whirlwind courtship' is the applicable cliché.

Gunther's house rebuilt, full of brand-new kitchens and bathrooms and guestrooms and lots to eat and drink. (That was not this house – and where is it, this house? In the country but how far into the country? We are not in Arnsburg: where am I?) Gunther jovial, prosperous, glowing. Barbara adult and poised, happy and confident, delighted to show her former lover that the pretty little draggletail was now a real woman; a very good unassuming hostess as well as an exemplary housewife, and plainly an excellent mother to that nice little boy, who was open and well-mannered . . . the only shadow seemed to be that Barbara had had no further children.

And there was Sibylle, now grown up and a university student. Shy still, soft-spoken, not much to say for herself. Talk about falling like a sack-of-bricks. 'Of course I remember you,' blushing just a little. She was not really 'pretty'; nothing like Barbara had been and indeed still was (no overblown peonies there, despite the healthy appetite for beer); but immensely, overwhelmingly attractive. And both of them – I mean both Gunther and Barbara – openly delighted with the tremendous unabashed attack upon this awkward girl (silent, one would almost call it withdrawn).

Not that it was anything to make a fuss about. Gunther, lighting a cigar – one of his few indulgences; how nice that 'nowadays one can get good ones' – got confidential.

"They've a good relationship. I worried a bit at first. Child very devoted to me, all she had y'know, and all that, and not much age difference between them really, might she get all jealous and possessive? Well, not a bit; they've always been comfortable together. With you, perhaps a bit of residual fear. A young child in the bad years, just at the most impressionable, old enough to register and understand some pretty horrible experiences – people trapped in cellars, people with their lungs exploded by blast. Remembers you in your uniform; Jesus-christus, that's a Terror Flieger. But you and I always got on well enough, didn't we, and she trusts me. Doesn't care a damn what people would say now. Myself I'm all for it – heals old wounds. There'd be a few of the neighbours glowering and muttering; we'll none of us pay any attention."

Barbara when he went to help with the washing-up (a good moment for a nice chat) was equally without complex.

"Youh, my step-daughter, and she's hardly younger than I am! ''S'allright dear, she's gone out for a walk, commune with the forest and the wolves, no worry, she knows how to look after herself. As I did – ha ha ha. We've never had any problems. Think how it might have grated on us both, and it never did. Watch those glasses, duck, they're horribly fragile and they cost the earth. When good-ol-sex rears its ugly head, yours wasn't ugly, my pet, it was perfectly sweet, she might jam her legs together a bit, don't worry my lips are sealed, but she'll get to know pretty quick what it took me no time at all to find out and that is you're a bit of a bastard upon occasion but you're mostly a kind and considerate person, because if you weren't then my good old Gunther wouldn't have much time for you and you'd get these freezing looks, y'know, always beautifully polite but a hard frost and your dick drops off in the night. Bless you, lamb, we got through that in no time, let's go and do some boozing."

Well, yes, there had been a good deal of get-your-hand-off-my-bra-strap.

But Sibylle and he had more in common than they knew. Five years difference, that seems a lot when you're young but they were both 'pre-war children'. Both had been strictly brought up (Robert had been the kind of Englishman who carried little bits of string in his pockets and complained about excessive use of lavpaper). Both had known the depression – never forget, said Gunther, that the Führer appeared to have the answer to unemployment. The war years, and the rationing. Both of them detested waste and refused ever to throw away bread (the way the French waste bread!). Sibylle darned and patched long after they were comfortably off, not to say rich. She had never been able to abide 'servants' and to this day, he was quite sure, could be found on her knees, polishing. Very German? The same thing used to be said about Marlene, that she liked scrubbing floors? There is probably a grain of truth in it.

Memories – admit, unworthy, but one wasn't about to feel ashamed. Barbara's knickers coming down in a few hayfields – that had been a greengage-summer, and there were punts too on the little rivers of the Ruhr land, to be borrowed from men who found a pike or a perch a good answer, in those days when sausage was meagre. Sibylle's knickers did not come down. But there were plenty of fibres in the cord that, already, bound them. He would say now that behind his absurd likes-and-dislikes there was a deep crack of insecurity. And this was a girl who possessed and who promised security.

That is, remains, a truth. But I have been rambling. About these putative grandchildren – yes, of course it is possible and perfectly likely. Simply, it never occurred to me. The little boy, Rainer – none of us, call it tact, call it the respect we felt for one another, ever mentioned, ever breathed a word. We knew that this was my child, whom Gunther had rescued, and nothing remained to be said. I was of course quite horribly egoist from beginning to end. There was much about that new Germany I did not greatly like; I never wished to make a home there. I put indeed a great deal of pressure upon Sibylle to forget it, never to go back. For years I didn't, and out of loyalty – doubtless – neither did she: I think we both felt that this page should not be turned back, and it never was. I am sure that Gunther understood this. They sent occasional brief notes, Christmas card sort of things. Never photos nor 'reminiscences'.

Very Brit I was then: still am. As I got older it got worse. I have been these forty years a European but have never lost my accent, nor the irritating mannerisms, which both amused and infuriated Sibylle.

They had lived in England awhile. In Italy too and in Paris.

The boy brought him his lunch. Boys? – both were in their later twenties but this the younger of the two and somehow the more sympathetic. A more open look; the other had a sour, sullen expression. One could see they were brothers – he could be no judge of a 'family' look! The elder was the taller, darker hair, a heavy, shaved jaw; this one fair-haired – something of Barbara in the look? But one must make a start.

"I owe you an apology. I hear you are my grandchild, I hope you know I had no realisation of that.

"I should wish at least that we can learn to understand each other better. This silence – it doesn't serve much purpose. I am quite an old man now, and I dislike losing time; as much I suppose as I dislike false positions." At least he didn't just storm out of the door and slam the bolts.

"I spoke for a moment with my wife. I didn't know about that, either. She's of course your aunt. In one sense too your granny; it's a complicated sort of relationship."

The boy did say something then, if as though sucking on a lemon. "Yes. My Tante Sibylle. She's like our mother."

This was news! "You can't object to telling your name?"

"My name is Christian. My brother is Joachim. All right? Eat your dinner," absurdly like Sibylle, "before it gets cold. There's a piece of cheese if you want it. French cheese," sarcastically, going out. But wasn't it a start? He didn't mind eating cheese; he could take it or leave it; ate it wishing only there were a glass of wine to go with it. A 'liking for stale bread and German mineral water', he had built fictional characters upon less. But this was not fiction! Even if he were reminded of the marvellous episode in Dumas – the Fiend Lady de Winter captured and imprisoned by her brother!

The 'Second Day of Imprisonment'! He could remember five, after that the drama accelerates. An omen? John liked to tell himself that he was not in the least superstitious: the lady is, though. Aware – one has to be – of the dangers in a withdrawal from reality he knew that he had been becoming increasingly withdrawn for some time now. Perhaps from the moment of that original shock, running down the road to ask old Poirier for reassurance . . . something odd is happening; is this real? Real people; Brigitta was real enough and so are my children. But could one call Daffodil real, by any definition? I have got into a fantasy world here, in which my imagination plays me tricks. Sibylle, and she is real enough, spoke of bringing me back, of making me real. Funny ways she chooses of going about it.

I was captivated in childhood, sure enough. D'Artagnan is like Aladdin or Sinbad, one of the enduring ones. I read this aloud to the children, and they too were mesmerised. Surely any child would be, even today? – although I first read it at perhaps ten years old, in a ridiculous slovenly English translation, depriving it of oxygen – and bowdlerised into the bargain! Which I never realised; some Victorian worthy thought it unsuitable for healthy little

boys that d'Artagnan should have got into bed with Milady
(not to speak of her maid).

This episode is admirably well made. The frightful
woman lands at Portsmouth with the instruction at all costs
to prevent the Duke of Buckingham from coming to the
rescue of La Rochelle, besieged by Cardinal Richelieu. She
is neatly captured, and imprisoned in a fortress, under the
guard of an incorruptible young man. The talented
actress – and seductive young woman – sets at once to work
to corrupt him! It suggests a parallel to John's imagination.

John used to laugh: both with – and with due humility at
his old friend – Monsieur Simenon, being by twenty-five
years his elder, as well as so far beyond him in fame and distinction! One of the old boy's more endearing traits had
been his generosity to young writers.

Over the years a tremendously elaborate machinery
had been built up, mightily impressive to visiting journalists – and marvellous copy. The preparations for
'withdrawal from reality' were in themselves a magnificent myth – Dumas, whom the old man loved, could have
done no better. They became legendary. Invitations were
refused, the doctor summoned, the blood pressure taken,
before the enclosure into purdah. All the day-by-day
details were then lovingly constructed: the filling of the
pipes and the sharpening of the pencils; the envelopes
for the framework and the Paris phone directory for the
names . . .

All true, he said (playing with the golden ball, itself the
perfect totem), perhaps (laughing heartily) just a little
exaggerated, but the press, you know, loves it. And you
know, cher confrère, it isn't stupid.

Very much not so. Like other mannerisms; the 'never
reading anybody else's books'. (Perfectly untrue, but this
saves ever having to say how bad they are, which upsets les

braves gens.) Or the utter refusal to allow alterations, even of a comma, by printers or copy-editors. 'Give them half a chance they think they wrote the book themselves.' (Publishers are much inclined to this delusion.) But in this instance, the frontier between fiction, which is truth, and reality, which is not, needs these careful barriers.

Goethe's *Dichtung und Wahrheit* was one of the old boy's favourite sayings. Fiction is truer than reality.

Am I losing sight of my apprehensions of truth? Sibylle says . . . "This will not do." No. Talking to oneself out loud won't do either.

How do these realities fit with Sibylle's truths? She does not wish for violence, which is contrary to all her principles. This kidnapping, sequestration, is the work of these young men.

My grandchildren! The family relationship is a complicated one. Through Gunther's adoption of Barbara's son, my son, their father, Sibylle is their aunt. Since she is still my wife she is also a sort of step-grandmother to them. That sounds unreal, but it is the truth. Between herself and them is a tight, close-knotted bond.

Towards myself their behaviour has been very violent indeed. Short of knocking me down, tying me up, holding my feet to the fire, difficult to imagine worse. Why? What is their motivation?

One can only guess. Their attachment, devotion to her is real enough and understandable. Their father – who has certainly abandoned them and is perhaps no longer alive – that could be a source of bitterness and anger, which they project. Their mother; it is possible that she is unknown to them. Theorising ahead of my data, ain't I, but it makes for some coherence. Sibylle has of course good reason for showing bitterness, and her grief . . .

Speculating, John, and that is foolish.

This damned cell, I cannot even pace it up and down, it is too small. My feet are glued to the floor, as my mind is glued to this senseless, squirrelling gallop around and around, getting nowhere. The exercise bicycle is only another manner; the running feet pursue the running mind.

To say that Sibylle – to suggest that any woman – has no propensity towards extreme violence is absurd and plain untrue. Mr Pepys (John's companion ever since returning from England) is proof to the contrary. He got an awful fright, the good man. Several days after the fearful show-down with Elizabeth, just as he is thinking that at the price of much and salutary humiliation he has made his peace with her, he is perturbed by her refusal to come to bed and staying up instead with much brooding and muttering in another room. Not much he can do but go to bed him-self – when suddenly the curtains are flung aside and dear God, there she is coming at him with a homely household implement, the tongs, and she has made the ends, the claws, red-hot, and nobody ever got out of bed quicker. Yes, an episode in high comedy. Not, though, for Elizabeth, and yes, also, yes, one can perfectly well imagine Sibylle . . . She is, perhaps, a little less spontaneous. John doesn't know. He doesn't know. I don't know. There are things here that nobody knows.

No, I don't think it unheard-of. Nothing inherently unlikely. Even the tongs – in today's country cottage no fea-ture more prized than the open fireplace and the père Poirier's pride and joy, his birch and apple logs autumn-cut and three years in stock. Given a squabble at the domestic hearth, the woman-scorned, blood on fire, behaves exactly like the Elizabeth three hundred years before . . . John, are you trying to be funny?

The preparation, the deliberation, the delay; can one

accept that these young men are only the instruments of some long-matured vengeance? Preposterous. Even the language is a parody of Byronic melodrama.

It is still possible that something long-dormant in Sibylle, has met and quickened a stifled, smouldering terror within these boys. Oh yes, such things happen. But what is the use of speculating? Perhaps, John, there might be a means of escape.

One of my fragments of military lore not yet quite obliterated is that a soldier's first duty is to escape. This is not the same as 'Bandit, Bandit!' jargon. 'My Cock is Strangled', 'Flash your Weapon' and such like amusements: I remember it being told me that whatever I forgot in later life 'you never forget your last three' – the digits of course of one's Army number.

So fuck Lady de Winter (pious sentiment); she has nothing to do with this. But perhaps with the means. I'm not about to dig any tunnels. Her technique of corrupting the guardian takes time. I can feel my life getting smaller, and this four-walled space which encloses me is also within me. This door is bolted; that door which was mine, leading to the world outside, which I could pass whenever I chose, closes upon me. It pinches me now, so that I have ado to breathe. When it shuts I shall hear it; the last thing I shall hear.

So push back, John, while you still can.

The boy Christian also brought my supper, and this seemed a good omen since there's no doubt at all that he's much more amenable than his shovel-jawed brother – about whom there's something odd and I haven't worked out what it is; there's more in that face than determination and a sort of sullenness. In those deepset eyes . . . Whereas about the younger of my grown-up grandsons (too ridiculous) there is something open and spontaneous; can it be humour? Could I once get him to admit the absurdity, the farcical comedy, of this – this sequestration. The human being, any human being, is capable of every madness. The writer imagines many; a great many more are unimaginable, until they happen. Across the years of living with Sibylle, and loving her, make no mistake, I learned and painfully never to be surprised. A man will stop at something. A woman will not.

So, as the old joke has it, of the pedantic husband and the adulterous wife, 'You, my dear, are surprised. I am merely astonished.' And not even that, now, that I've got used to the idea. I am going to act 'astonished'.

"Is this your grandfather's house? He lived in the town when I knew him."

"Yes, you were friendly, weren't you. His brother's." There was no harm in telling me, now.

"Christian, I'm sorry, but this soup is stone cold, you know."

"Give it me, I'll warm it up. It's no trouble."

A pointer? He is thinking that a peaceful – a reasonable – solution will be found? He made sure the bolts were drawn, though.

"That's better, I hope." And staying to see that it was. And curious too, to know how I'm taking the situation.

"Burningly so, thank you. Does your father live here too?"

"No." Flat.

"A pity. I wish I knew him."

"You aren't likely to, now." (What does that mean?) "You were the English officer. You made a child, and abandoned it." What has Barbara told them? Surely Gunther would never –

"That's not quite true, you know. Did your mother –"

"I never knew my mother."

"That is curious. We have that in common; neither did I."

"I'm not going to talk about it. My father is dead."

"I'm very sorry indeed. I couldn't have known. Maybe I should have. That is a great shock."

"I mustn't stop."

I had planned for a remark like this. I was going to try a bit of gentle irony. 'Nobody's going to think I've overpowered you.' Putting some comic emphasis to sting him into staying awhile. And this overpowered me. I sat there looking at my hardly touched soup, at a half-eaten piece of bread and butter, a fine appetite I had now for all that. Slices of sausage, jam on a saucer, a glass of milk. I wanted a bloody great jolt of malt whisky. I needed a cigarette, very badly. I needed to scream and shout. Hadn't the stomach even for that. After a long time I got up and put the tray with the cold soup down by the door. Stick to routine. Leek and potato too, very good and a favourite of mine. Sibylle would know that, she who never forgot anything. It wasn't likely to have been in the forefront of her mind.

I lay on the bed. The bed was too soft. I lay on the floor instead. Stretched straight out, hands behind my head. Put you in a coffin, they'll give you a little pillow. Pious people put a crucifix in your folded hands. The more classically minded, a copper coin. To pay the ferryman. It is time for me too, to take the ferry. That was a phrase of Robert's, current in his time. So-and-so died, one said he'd 'taken the ferry'. Strange, I used to do this often in younger days. Didn't like divans, sofas. The straight floor rested me, and was quite soft enough. Tired. I haven't done this for many years. After a hard day, once one began to unwind, would turn on my front. Get one of the children to 'do my back'. Jaimie, the bugger, would always demand a bribe. Sixpence for ten minutes – would stop on the dot, too. The little ones were kinder-hearted. Alan was good at it. Cathy in her girl's way, less strength in the fingers but made up by her own special technique. One gave them the sixpence anyhow, naturally. Sibylle had long, strong, finely formed hands; still has them. No good for creature-comforts. Too hard; too insensitive. Too impatient perhaps, always in a hurry. Skilled, in their way; like any German girl of that generation trained to be careful, meticulous with a needle and thread. Wasn't so much that we were poor but one did not allow waste. Children tore off buttons, ripped their shirts. She knitted too, skilfully but badly because always in a hurry. Forever having to rip three rows to get back to the fault. Like Penelope. It would take a long time before anything got finished.

Not true, to say 'insensitive'. When I was very tired, and unless they have known and lived with writers, no one ever realises, they think it's 'easy'; they don't know, and cannot see, that it's identical to a day down the mine. One comes up at the end of the shift, blinking at the daylight, black from head to foot, thinking only of a shower and clean things, and getting back to a wife, and the children. And soup, and bread-and-butter. One picks up then, enough to look at the children's homework. And when they are quiet at last, washed and in their pyjamas, to read to them.

I would be too tired, sometimes, even to stand under the shower. Lie there, feeling beaten, aching. Sibylle would come quietly and sit by me. Her fingers would press gently upon my closed eyes. Between, on the congested sinus, on the pressure point at the top of the skull, above the fontanelle. She had never been taught but instinct told her. After a while – 'I must go and make the supper,' but sometimes (were the children out? or late back from school? what?) as I unwound, my hand might well have strayed up her skirt. One hadn't 'thought of anything'.

Aren't those the best moments, when energy suddenly slides back into one? I sat up, began to unbutton her blouse.

She might laugh, in self-conscious, irritated embarrassment. 'No; they'll come in, at any moment.' But she could, and luxuriously, want very badly indeed to be undressed.

Lying here on the floor, looking at the ceiling; as Pamela Widmerpool said in the same position, she is looking at a Tiepolo ceiling-painting of the Gyges legend, "Who's the naked man with the stand?" One does also have to say it's a pleasure not to find oneself impotent. I was not reminded of Daffodil; that's not a good comparison. Knowing that this corrupt little schoolgirl was in reality an accomplished porn-pro did not alter enjoyment: as one pretended, so she became. One cannot do that with real women like Sibylle.

It has cleared up to be a nice spring evening; what one can see of it from a skylight. English people hurrying home will say to one another, 'The days are drawing out,' with joy in the voices; This spring is going to be different; better than the others we have known. Jacques Brel could sing, *C'est dur, de mourir au printemps, tu sais*. Quite slowly it faded into night, and with night came quiet.

The third day of imprisonment.

The day comes too; this one clear and cloudless. I needed no clock. I was up, shaved, dressed, right on time. As I was cleaning toothpaste off the washbasin I heard the bolts drawn; puts one 'in a good mood'. Lovely smell of coffee. It was fresh, strong, very hot. Sibylle too looked trim, springy, clear-eyed. Her body has dried out with age. One notices the cords in her throat, between the points of a clean shirt-collar, but she was never one to get fat, despite complaints that eating cream cake put inches on her bottom. I'm much the same and glad of it; one would rather be stringy than cushiony. She is much gaunted but that brings her good bones into relief. The fine bridge of her splendid nose which Cathy has inherited, though hers is Roman rather than aquiline (both faces have distinction) was shiny; she has never used much make-up. A little round the eyes, a slash of lipstick on a wide thinnish mouth.

"Good morning, Sibylle," so that she had to smile at this cheerful voice even if it were the smile the teacher uses when putting a question to the backward child. Encouraging, expectant.

"You see, beginning to do you good, instead of all that drinking and those awful cigars you begin to think. You were disciplined enough about work until you got so self-indulgent."

Irritation wriggles in the grip of patience. I have so often heard this tirade, and invariably she got her timing wrong just as when imprudently one switches on the television while drinking coffee in the kitchen: the physical-fitness girls with their merciless clean teeth going, 'Higher, ladies, higher,' and never out of breath, so smugly disintoxicated.

"I've worked a few things out. Need more basic information. Is this your house?"

"Barbara's, after Father died. She didn't last much longer, alas. She got a cancer. We were like sisters. I'd promised that there'd always be a home, for the boys."

"And their father, what did he have to say about all this? Since you weren't, let's call it, Gunther's only child?"

"Yes, it's time you knew. Rainer – I'm always sad that I never knew him. He went away. What the village would call 'went to the bad'. I don't use such phrases," angrily. "And Father didn't either. Loyalty, support, exactly as one would expect, he was what the Jews call a Just – you know that?"

"I always liked him. You'd better tell me what happened."

"It's years ago. I wasn't around," giving me rather a look. "Father didn't speak of it. I gathered from Barbara what little I know. That he racketed about from one dodgy job to another. He had great charm . . . used up great energy in getting a job, and bored once they have it." One couldn't call her tone spiteful. Cutting it was, and it hurt.

"That he fathered two children on a girl none of us knew. In France it's legal for her to hide her identity. He deserted her of course. Father took the responsibility, to bring the children up in return for her surrendering her rights, and he would never say more."

"Except what happened to Rainer."

"Gunther", bleak, "decided it would be wrong to give you needless pain. Saying that if it were anyone's fault it was his own."

So I have written that down. If there's a hero, anywhere round here, Gunther is his name. So easy to go about muttering, 'Bad blood in that boy.' Like Robert's beastly sisters.

"He killed himself." Sibylle equally determined to stick to the facts. "As alas so many German boys do. Now that Barbara has gone too these boys see me as their mother. It's the least I can do. How many broken families are there in this sad country?"

"Not all of them my doing." Which I should not have said, though perhaps pain forced it out of me, and for once Sibylle kept her tongue. "Yes, Gunther was like that," I concluded, feebly.

"But it hardly explains why I should get shot at. Or why a man, who as far as I could see had the misfortune to look like me, was nearly killed."

Her expression did not change at all.

"As far as I know," slowly, "Barbara told them no more

than that their father was your son. They know to be sure that I was – am – your wife."

"Barbara did not hate me."

"And nor do I. Nor do I. You must grasp that I came late on the scene. Eight years ago they were just out of their teens. One doesn't know, ever, what children get in their heads. I can promise you that I haven't filled them with anger against you."

I felt sure that this was true. "In all justice, I suppose that your appearance in their midst would only harden whatever grievance towards me they imagine. There's a sort of fatality at work. But why this, this violence, this absurd kidnapping?"

"I was trying to make them see that what started, I believe, as an elaborate trick – it would be comic to make you frightened – was altogether wrong and bad."

I should have gone on, patiently disentangling. I made a bad mistake; I began to get angry. Is it my unhappy gift or hers? Some such phrase as 'flicked on the raw'? One had so often the sensation with her of salt rubbed in.

"So now they can see for themselves what kind of beast I am. Brit, into the bargain. Germans can live in peace with the French whom we invaded three times within a hundred years; with the Poles whom we've been invading for a thousand. But the eternal enemy goes on slipping the knife in, wittering on about us being still all nazis, these aphorisms they think profound, that we're either at their feet or their throats. Brits boasting, as they always do, at their most abject. Can anyone be surprised at what these young Germans feel when this shit is forever being poured in their ears? I have to suffer for it, I was the arrogant young filth who raped their grandmother. Gunther knew better, but what could he do, an old man, after you came here telling everyone I'm such a shit you left me."

She didn't give way to anger.

"I have never told them anything. You are not a bad man even when you are a weak one. They'll get to know you, you'll have plenty of opportunity to explain yourself."

So write this down too, will you. Instead of correcting my mistakes I make them worse still. Isn't that the fatality of so many couples, the infernal getting one's own back, like a lot of stupid Corsicans. I could watch myself – could see John back-sliding . . .

"So you can justify all this to yourself as you always do. You always were good at coming out the injured party. So you encouraged them to burn my house, little miss Never-in-the-wrong."

Her eyes got larger; that's all. "What distorted notions, unhappily unfair, their father and, I must suppose, their mother too put into their heads is none of my doing. Gunther marrying Barbara was right and good and so I thought at the time and my marrying you would be right too. I was a young girl and totally innocent. I did not know what you would do to me."

She was always quick-tempered. An absurd memory – that horrible English habit of teasing, while claiming that nobody else ever has any sense of humour . . . Long ago; her first baby, yes, Jaimie, had some small childish ailment. I forget what; nothing to worry about, touch of infantile diarrhoea? Really it was to take the drama out; she was fussing needlessly and I wanted to make her laugh. 'Your baby's gone down the plughole.' In Cockney. She thought it was mockery. 'Poor little thing, so nasty and thin' . . . Burst into a flood of tears and I was awkwardly taken aback. 'You shit, you awful shit.' Only a stupid joke and she never forgot it. 'Tu es dégueulasse,' – commonplace phrase, 'you make me throw up.' She meant it literally; she did throw up, poor girl.

What I did to her; this tirade I have heard a hundred times. My Englishness, the snobberies and superiorities. That I had contempt for her unformed mind, for her Germanness, for countrified ways, provincialities, homely ways and traditions. True, alas, such a lot of it. I am greatly ashamed to think of the contemptuous arrogance I brought to so much of our early life, the efforts to prop my self-esteem; I had little enough confidence in my strength and capacities. It is certain that Sibylle suffered for this.

The Paris of those days – the city was as full as ever it had been of the ferment of the entire world, the artists and intelligentsia, the Poles and Czechs, the Russians and Hungarians, all of whom had lost so much to the invading devouring sterilising maw of the Third Reich. We aren't talking about Jews here, but about families broken and possessions lost, homes destroyed and jobs snapped off, careers and hopes and ambitions. Whatever had happened it was simpler and more consoling, and more understand-able, that Germans should bear the blame. The French were sore and ashamed at themselves. So many had wel-comed the occupier and fallen over their own feet collaborating. Clouds of intensely complicated philosoph-ical explanation went into whitewashing the ignoble. The English had at least stood up and fought for themselves. The old bloody-minded obstinacy stood us in good stead there. We did it for the worst reasons very often – when indeed there were any reasons; most the familiar isola-tionist instinct, 'No Popery' all over again. None of this was of any help to Sibylle. Wherever we went she felt that fin-gers were pointing at her and very often she was right. In those years I did not mention my own German mother.

Far too long and too often I nourished myself with pre-judice and propaganda. When it came to the early years of the European concept it was the vision and courage of

Monnet and Robert Schuman we admired; it was fashionable to dismiss Adenauer as a 'provincial mayor'. My personal cowardice went deeper still. I didn't want Sibylle 'going home' even on brief visits, and invented every pretext to raise difficulties, and she gave in, poor girl: the stubbornness and sullenness of later years had their roots here in the time of my being 'Parisian', when too the children were small and Sibylle stayed at home and did her own scrubbing, refusing often to set foot in houses where Germany would be denigrated, and all things German dismissed with contempt in which I so often acquiesced.

The tirade now was so familiar, I didn't even listen. Can't you invent something new, I used to sigh. We tried very hard, both of us, to clean the sticky treacle off our wings. Here and now I had nothing but silence to offer. All the words had been said so often and to so little purpose. Jaimie has never forgiven me of course. Alan, Cathy – they were younger, and had more sense of humour as well as objectivity.

She walked out finally, and slammed the door. It left me bitter and confused. Had neither of us then learned any better, even now?

That bloodshot Joachim brought the lunch tray, glowering; no doubt had seen Sibylle 'upset', which wouldn't improve his feelings towards me. I dropped a few conversational seeds, but that is stony ground.

And there is still that something more, which nags at me and which I cannot bring home. Is the little bugger – he isn't above fifteen centimetres taller than I am – on some kind of dope? Setting down what I know, and that's precious little, I'd doubt the classic heavy stuff. Needles, flames, messing with spoons; big innocent though Sibylle is, she'd know, the brother would be bound to know. There's cannabis, smoked it myself in the old days, we used only to get three per cent and the Dutch, a clever folk with plants, are said now to get ten. Which would give a powerful impetus – can't rule that out but would it make one aggressive and unpredictable in this sort of way? Speed sounds to me much more likely. Last time I was in the States, the West Coast – metamphetamines were a big worry, more than the sinsemilla, one gets these appalling reactions – is there a lot of that here?

There's that stuff in England with a name like marzipan, legally prescribed but a flourishing black market, creating ravages among teenagers in Glasgow. And to be sure there's ecstasy, another Dutch speciality and that might be likeliest since we're not at all far from the Dutch border. My cop friends tell me it's less dangerous; it's also widespread, being fairly cheap – a synthetic, and the chemistry is not all that tricky.

I can sound learned with this jargon – THC and MDMA. The fact is that I know very little indeed about it. I have never used this flashy kind of detail in a book. It sounds good at the time and a year later it's out of date. From what I do know, the ephedrine derivatives which, very loosely, we've been calling 'speed' these last twenty years, sound to me a likely sort of explanation. An all-too-frequent pathology, about which the police, the legal authority, and all social workers, are pretty tight-lipped. The habit of all politicians, to treat anything in the least serious as though not to be mentioned in front of the children, finally getting an effect the exact opposite of that intended, since anything mysterious, dangerous or forbidden creates an attraction.

It has been another lovely day. I am suffering. How long do I have to stay barred into this minute space, subject to this crippled, malformed – here, too, the effect will be the opposite of that 'intended'. Crouching here, I do not get bigger but smaller, I do not become better but more evil. I see nothing but sky, cloud, the passage of day towards night. I hear little. Sounds of traffic not far away, the odd plane or helicopter, the occasional mumble of indistinct voices, a car door slamming, meaningless clashes or jangles. Outside is Germany. The beautiful German spring. In the morning, standing by the skylight, I can smell the spring, it is April. I tried to stand on the exercise bike, to see out. One foot on the saddle and one of the handlebar, I gave it up, it was too difficult, I was too afraid of falling and breaking a bone. I am old and my sense of balance is not good.

I don't feel too bad physically. I have thought up a lot of movements to try and keep muscles supple, I do deep breathing. Not smoking, not drinking, this helps too. It is my mind that shrivels, stiffens. All day, today, there was sun. No clouds at all, scarcely any wind; anti-cyclone weather.

As it moved towards evening (the slope of the roof is easterly and I see only a morning sunlight; the beautiful westering is denied me) I must take refuge in memory, and inside imagination. I think of my house, a burned shell. The Peartrees are waiting for me to come back, to start reacting, to begin anew. I am sure that the père Poirier is – faithfully – keeping the garden from degenerating into jungle: an hour of an evening to cut the grass, to keep the more aggressive weeds at bay. He will deadhead the tulips.

Let me concentrate. The stones of that land are grey to the casual onlooker (those stones with which, so laborious and loving, I built the walls of terracing). I know them so well. Some are bluish; they can turn to indigo. But the subtleties of light, here . . . after rain, and when the westering sun slants, they go pink; the faded, soft venetian rose of old brocades and velvets, of weathered, sun-faded aquarelle paintings. In the evening light these pinks strengthen, are more pronounced.

Of course one can't write about colours. 'The lids of Juno's eyes' – he came close. Nauseated, one looks at rows of adjectives. Painters can't either; vile chemical pigments. In primitives, perhaps. Madonnas with rose-trees, bowls of lilies. The flowers in old oriental carpets. Latin poetry. Everywhere else, More equals Less. When I say that at twilight the stones are blue, grey, pink, mauve, and violet I have said nothing at all. When I say it's nearly May, will soon be June – twilight makes the irises, the azaleas, glow intensely, magically, what have I said? – adverbs are even worse. At least today's writers have learned at last to skip those dreadful laboured similes; everything had to be like something else. Back to Horace, Ausonius, where less is more. But you can't stop my lying on the floor to look at my patch of evening sky, thinking that my irises will soon be out. Alongside an ancient, simple, climbing rose, kind old Marguerite Hilling who can never make up her mind what tones and tints of pink she really is, and so generously paints them all.

Smelling the evening I can smell my mornings; while the sun rises the scents lie richest. A week or so – it was last summer but a week or ten months are alike 'ago' – a half-grown fox cub was on the top terrace scrabbling for a mouse, maybe. He didn't know enough to be frightened at seeing me; thought of running away but his mind on breakfast. Where is your mother? Has Peartree shot her? I have a pine marten too; they like houses.

The boy Christian brought my supper. He's a history student. We had a little chat about Otto von Bismarck. About whom I know next to nothing, but he knows a lot and that's the point.

"He invented black velvet." My contribution.

"What's that?"

"You mix stout and champagne." Give me a day or so more. 'Friendly' he isn't. I am sorely handicapped. I am the Brit, the cold egoist, the calculator, the false and the treacherous. And his grandfather. It will not be easy.

These boys, these girls, the students of today's Germany, are my great hope. I don't think we've much chance, but we've some. Petronius, in Nero's time, saw very little hope for Rome. It was very much as it is now; nobody thought of anything but money. In England they hate us – the Teutons, the Prussians.

Listen to some Schubert, shall we? I couldn't sing a note out loud, but in my head it's true, perfectly in key and rhythm, exact on the note – which I cannot even read. Of course I couldn't do complex orchestral pieces, instrumental harmonies. Only a simple melodic line for a voice, or – I like to think of Kleiber, out walking in the woods, working on the sixth symphony of Beethoven, the second movement 'by the brook', and listening to all the little streams running down the hillside – 'No no, that one's not in tune either.'

I moved the bed, to see my patch of night sky. There was a miracle. A great big full moon, sailing so stately and indifferent to the smoky wisps of hurrying cloud. Artemis has lit her crystal lamp. There is a lovely Latin song, '*Dum Dianae vitrea* . . .' I cannot, I cannot remember it, I am old but I am so ignorant, I went to a 'proper' school in England but the wonderful Virgil was badly taught, the Pious Aeneas poisoned our childhood, the pious pedagogues suppressed Dido – she felt, you see, physical passion, and that would never do.

So that it was hereabout, again, that I began to catch a

glimpse. No no, not Gunther! – his schooling hadn't included Virgil. An old man, Landgraf – his name escapes me – acting as Burgermeister of a little town his family had owned, because there wasn't anybody else. Nearly eighty but the habit of authority still there, in the sense of responsibilities – that, that was like Gunther. He it was who quoted me the line about burned Troy, kindly, smiling at the little boy dressed-up in officer's uniform –

'*Incensa Danai dominantur in urbe.*' And taught me the words for the Stunde Null, Germany's zero-hour. I had just enough Latin for that.

'*Una salus victis nullam sperare salutem.*' Those words I haven't forgotten. One security for the conquered is to hope for none.

I don't know why – yes I do, Schubert and a line of Latin, running together in my memory, bringing me back to schooldays, childish days, pre-war days. 1938 it must have been. 'Munich' meant nothing to us as children; it was the year of Ella Fitzgerald singing, 'A tisket, a tasket, my little yellow basket,' on the gramophone. And Richard Tauber came to England; quite a fuss about a distinguished Jewish refugee from nazi Austria. I thought him awful; cheap, meretricious. And one was quite, quite wrrrong. Television, only a month or so ago; collected clips, and a row of distinguished critics, English as well as German. Critics are such asses, they are so feeble and forever hedging, covering their bets in case they got it wrong. Comic now, this mighty praise.

"Accents one had never dreamed of . . . The most musicianly of singers . . . Not a great voice, no trumpet in it, but incomparably the finest ear . . . Incomparable Mozart voice, the most splendid Ottavio ever . . . And such a conductor! The Tales from the Vienna Woods as never before, and never since . . ." Dear God these futile words.

'Incomparable' – a glorious word, lovely descant; and so far below what one knows, what one hears.

But then for heaven's sake, why sing so much abject rubbish? Because, my dear boy, his range was simply enormous, because it isn't all that easy being a major artist and a tremendous romantic heart-throb, and being told you're a dirty little Jew and you better get the hell out of here while the going's good. You take your Austrianness with you, flaunting it, sentimentalising it, cheapening it. Just as I took all my Englishness with me, and might I remind you, Mr Charles, you have sicked up a lot of rubbish yourself in your life and what you call your career. Your Germanness you hid and were ashamed of.

It is a wonderful thing, being English. But one has to deserve it.

I have been filled with wonder in many unlikely places and at the oddest times, and under laughable circumstances. Astonishing people, the islanders, for would one not say this of Japan? Corsicans would say it of themselves, and with some justification – that potty little island to this day terrorises the Republic. One can be small, like Iceland or New Zealand, and be quite disproportionally remarkable. But England, which isn't Europe, isn't anything but itself and in such unlikely ways, so that born there, brought up there, one says Why me and Why here? Ireland, that other island we thought was ours too, is as extraordinary, but even there one wouldn't find Gladstone and Disraeli in the same room. It continues to mystify me. All countries are extraordinary and some of the smallest the most – look at Holland. But nowhere – certainly not Rome – did one find so much genius crammed into so petty, even so trivial, an area.

And look at us now. The rule, one must suppose, is that a people, and one can never quite make out what a 'people' consists of (what were Romans, who were Normans?), arrives on the scene and dominates the known world. And then they peter out. We lasted I suppose longer than most, and that I dare say is why we became the most arrogant of people. Now we are merely the most boastful, the world champion flag-flappers. Doesn't matter where you go, in Djakarta they're holding the Tiddleywink Games and at the rim of the arena will be a little, ludicrous gang waving Union Jacks and making more noise than any others. A sight Mr Gladstone would not have found edifying: we have become a universal laughing stock. Did we stop laughing at ourselves?

I can only speak for myself; I have enjoyed being English. Sibylle, never perhaps conspicuous for humour, did not laugh at me enough. My son Alan, in whom Englishness is strong, has never stopped finding me a figure of farce. I have been English in most corners of the world, wearing funny hats, unmistakable in voice and gesture, sympathetic on the whole, I should hope.

For I was persuaded that it wasn't enough. In Europe of all places the National thing, the Flag thing, was so pathetically obsolete. Seeing what the Third Reich had done, we thought we could do better. But I am as Alan tells me, the Old Man of Thermopylae – who never did anything properly.

Is it too late for me now? There is a German family here, in more ways than one 'mine'. I have been a conspicuous example of How Not To Do It; Gunther behind his façade of bureaucratic paper, of being the Postmaster from Prmsyl, did not worry about how to do it, but did it. His daughter is just the same. Hammered by me, mercilessly, all these years – Cathy saw, why did I not see – Sibylle's goodness gave way at last. Can I still? It is late, I must try to sleep, I want to be up early.

I got out of bed because the ragbag of my memory found another Latin line. Don't know rightly whose; Boethius or somebody.

> *Quae canit altis garrula ramis*
> *ales caveae clauditur antro.*

Not for me; I've only been here three days – the bird that sang in the high branches and is now locked in the cellar. I've been thinking of Sibylle as a young girl. She sang all day; she sang in my house as she had in Gunther's house. Bit by bit and so that one scarcely noticed it she sang less and it must be twenty years since I heard her singing.

If for myself a little, also; my high branches were books and they have burned. Wasn't that too one of the things for which we could never forgive the Goebbels crew – their burning of books?

Sibylle, come back, I'll write more books.

The Fourth Day. I'm not writing 'imprisonment' because I do not feel imprisoned. We're going to have a party. I wonder whether you've any champagne in the house. Don't worry if it's German – Sekt will do nicely. I got as close as I could to the skylight; the smell of morning is intoxicating. I am waiting for you. What's 'age' when all is said? You are sixty-five, when I count, and you're as slim, as light as when you were twenty. You won't have forgotten how to sing. You

Here the manuscript notebook breaks off.

Christian Kirchner

I don't want to be intrusive, clumsy. I thought, I hope carefully. It was my idea that I had no right to meddle with this. It ought to stay in the family. I should say straight off I went to see 'Alan', my 'uncle' in Paris, to ask his advice.

He showed me very much kindness. He asked me to stay for the weekend, with them in their home. They made me very welcome and I felt that. We talked together. He read the notebook.

Then it was he who gave me the address of my aunt, Catherine Charles, in Spain. He said she'd give me better advice than he could. Cathy, as she has told me to call her, isn't like an aunt, she isn't that much older and I find her like my sister. She's very much like her mother. I felt it easier to talk to a woman. There are things like sex men don't talk about together. Alan was right anyhow, I did not feel any shame or embarrassment talking with Cathy. She laughed a lot and she told me I need not hesitate. It was this last page in the notebook but it was all their private life. Cathy says she's sure I have got it right. That John at any age could never resist women but that his wife meant always more to him, physically too, than any other. But since I felt about Sibylle exactly like she was my own mother that was even more hard. Talking about her was like a sort of incest and there was an awful lot of incest already.

I trust Cathy's word. She says her mother was 'a very sexy woman' and after doing altogether without men for eight years, if John had asked her to go to bed she certainly would have said yes without any hesitating. If, that is. Well, you'll see. I've got that off my chest. I'm trying to write naturally, the way 'John' did. Isn't that last bit happy? He felt he had set himself free. After all the years of getting it wrong, of the schism, he was confident that he had come home. He had made up his mind and could see his path, it was going to be a renouncement, of the wrongs he had done her.

I don't find it easy to write. I envy the practised way he could throw loose thoughts on paper. It was his job, but I've no skill that way. I've got to have a shot and I hope you'll excuse my awkwardness. After all I didn't know him. I'd only just 'met' him. I thought I knew all about it, and found I knew so little.

The gap in age for a start, he was my grandfather and not far from fifty years between us. And she was my aunt and my granddad's wife, it sounds laughable. Cathy helped me to see her as a young woman, as John says 'singing all the time', Cathy didn't recall that but says it's true. I've told myself that 'age' has no importance. One sees history as now, as well as the however-many-centuries ago.

He uses 'I' but often 'John' of himself, so one sees this was a technical thing, that then he was more detached, and he talks about 'the two sides of his head'. So I'm using 'John' since the grandfather personage doesn't mean much to me. 'Sibylle' is easier since we used her name also. 'Tante' is German but she found it too formal for us. Jo and I saw her as our mother, which she was in every sense bar the physiological, since she adopted us. Well, most of my friends call their mother by her first name.

I have to tell what happened. I can't be *exact* because I wasn't there to write it all down.

The police did, though. A big report of many pages. They went over everything minutely, like after a fire for the insurance company. They want to feel sure they've got as near as can be to exactitude of timing, measurement. I saw how they work because I spent hours in the Kripo offices. They were polite, and quite open because I couldn't be a suspect, since I wasn't there. They do this, I suppose the same everywhere, and the report goes to the State's Attorney office even if then it's just filed, and they let me have a copy. They're human beings too. One doesn't like them, but they acted very straight to me and I have to give them credit.

So you understand, this is 'history', a reconstruction, how it must have been. I think John would say that 'reality' isn't truth. I can see how this could be so. Leastways, that when one doesn't 'know', the imagination of the artist could come closer to the truth than a heap of learned aridities resolute in rejecting anything not 'factually' documented. Thinking of an example so well known as 'Montaillou', we'd know nothing but for the Bishop of Pamiers being such a meticulous bastard, and all his holy Dominican clerks writing it all down in the most scrupulous detail. When the Highway Patrol measured it all, took photos, got eye-witnesses, put it all in 'procès-verbal' one can't get any closer to the truth. What happened here in the house is guesswork, but pretty well informed.

Looking at John's last pages he was so sure he had it all clear it was like he'd won the Lotto, not knowing there was a Fact he hadn't guessed at. It seems obvious. Any objective student would catch it quickly. Sibylle knew only after her father told her, and that was only when he was dying. That gave the item extra weight, built it up, into a drama. To that generation, and in these circumstances, a big tragic fatality. Happening to myself, or told me by a friend of mine, maybe even today we'd feel the shock. I don't think we'd go overboard. I can't tell. A historian would say, 'happens all the time', and a biologist, 'don't take it all that seriously'. But this word incest is frightening. Among all peoples it has always been the taboo. In so-called noble families they were forever marrying their cousins, and often got very badly interbred as a result. Right – Sibylle was John's sister.

I can write it down impartially if not impersonally then historically. But to them a thunderbolt. Not my field, and I know nothing about it, but didn't the Pharaohs marry their sisters?

John knew nothing, it's plain, until that last morning. Sibylle hadn't known for long. Gunther, it's pretty evident, hadn't wanted ever to tell her, felt it his duty to keep quiet, and we know what duty meant to him. He must have decided at the end that she had to know, since she was no longer living with John. But how had he got to know about this, her dreadful secret, poor Sibylle? I think it can only have been through hiring detectives. It's the sort of thing they do. They don't care. It is through the miseries of others that their pockets are lined. Gunther's thoughts became suspicions, and then he could not rest until – how long had he known, keeping quiet?

In the notebook there are traces. There when he was a young officer with the occupation troops, Gunther asked about his name. But 'Charles' is not an uncommon name, and if one had a penny for the thousands of women in Germany called Magda – longish odds, one would say. If we all knew our genealogies. When people lived in the same village,

191

generation after generation, cousinage got very complicated. A great many of us now can't get further than a grandfather 'came out of the East', and with church and municipal records burned or bombed as often as they were, most of us never will. And might be astonished.

Trying to look historically, even inside two generations it's only a coincidence made possible by the timing of pre- and post-war. John's mother married an Englishman, a banal happening. This marriage breaks up or got broken. Early thirties, she was a young woman and John a small child. It follows naturally that when she found an opportunity to remarry she took it.

So John was English and Sibylle was German. Nobody would think twice about this, either. Only this absurd behaviour as though one were white and the other black.

For myself, I can't speak for poor Jo, it's no more than saying 'Oh, bad luck.' It happens often enough in football, player puts it through his own goal. I don't find it more than a small, quite a narrow coincidence that John should be sent here by the Army. This was the British Sector. How many young soldiers got dumped here, and how many slept with German girls? Nothing untoward about Gunther marrying Barbara to give her child a home and a father. The only exceptional, extraordinary thing is that it was John's child.

Bits of driftwood come down with the current. One sticks on a stone in the brook, sets up an eddy, into which others fall. And they glue together. On a big scale they'd call it a logjam. Sometimes they couldn't break it up, they would have to dynamite it. These things in history, some people see them as a conspiracy, it couldn't have happened by accident, it's too neat, happening just at that spot, it must have been planned by malevolence. My brother, Joachim, was like that, he used to get into rages thinking it was done on purpose with malice aimed at himself. Paranoia? He began to think that somehow he'd been deprived of his human rights, his very identity, and it was through the fault of the English, of his English grandfather. He came to see life as a battle between himself and all the world. He was brilliant, a much better student than myself. Those pills, when one has been eating speed for any length of time, I think a court would accept the notion of an induced insanity. You have to see his point of view. I've been talking too much about myself.

What I believe, Cathy thinks too it must have been so, the police accept. John asked, suggested, the form doesn't matter, Sibylle to go to bed with him. We can't tell, the incest idea came up and suddenly choked her. We think she ran away, panicked off blindly. And didn't bolt the door because it wasn't forced.

John escaped. We don't know any details. On impulse, since he left, or plain forgot, his clothes, his washing things. Took only his bag, the things a man always carries. And the notebook. One imagines that he didn't 'think', any more than Sibylle 'thought'. Escaping was instinct. A soldier's duty. Anything like 'crept out' is speculation, nor does it matter. They can't have noticed. Busy quarrelling? As they did, a lot. Jo loved her, as I did and more, and perhaps too much. He would try to – I don't know the word – settle, console. But not 'reason with'. John might have wished or tried for that. Not with Joachim there.

Probably the first thing they heard was the car. Jo hadn't done anything with it at all but put it away in the old cart shed. Even the key was still in the ignition. John escaping had never been part of any scenario. Oldish, perfectly good car. The motor might well have roared a bit with his accelerating it, nervous. That would have brought them running out. Nobody knows, but for the marks on the ground.

Jo had one of those Japanese things, four-wheel-drive, high, square and full of gadgets. Stupid thing I thought it, and told him so, but it was the apple of his eye. Powerful, macho, people get out of the way, as I dare say you know. Big brutish bars fore and aft, lots of lamps hung on them. I wish to say that my brother was not like this. I am tall and strong. He outdid me two centimetres both ways, and he didn't have to show off his maleness. I have to say the thing amused me, too, and I borrowed it sometimes. My girl hated it.

The road needs some explaining. Around us is a maze of twisty little country roads, but the Autobahn is only five kilometres off, and the access is well signalled. This John would have followed naturally, and driving pretty fast.

The detail interested the police. Jo drove that thing like God's wrath, and of course knew the roads blindfold. Whereas John, an old man, and shaky, might not have been totally prudent but wasn't intending to kill himself. So we think that Sibylle argued, and held Jo back as much as she could. She would have wanted John to get away? Everything is arguable, and none of it matters. Sibylle was in the truck. And they didn't catch him up before the autobahn entrance.

Witnesses said Jo passed them doing anything up to a hundred-and-eighty and rough with it, flashing lights and breathing down their neck. We have a lot of accidents on our fast roads, and virtually all of them from sheer brutal egoism. Going too fast, getting too close and not giving a damn for others. Once more, my brother was not like this in his real nature. The speed-pills were explanation enough for the police.

The Kripo officer, at his desk, with the Highway patrol's report in front of him, and two cans of no-alcohol beer, pushed one over to me with the medical, sheets of it, but the paragraph about traces-of-amphetamines scored through with a yellow marker-pen. If I had tried to tell him about Jo's character he wouldn't have listened. Why should he?

I wasn't feeling 'shocked' by then. It was two days later. Just bitterly hurt, myself smashed-up. I know I wanted to ask about the clowns one sees, you will have them too, doing one-seventy while chatting on their mobile phones, eating their vanity-pills. What's the use? He'd have said, impatiently, I-know-I-know. There are people who jeer. Yaa-ah, moralising. This is their crushing insult, that one is being Angelic. I don't have any quotes from writers, the way John did, but I do remember a line from an English poem, and I think it's Doctor Johnson. Here something-something tumbles on your head (a roof tile maybe?) 'And there a female atheist talks you dead.' It's about London but we've plenty too.

I suppose I hardly need tell you about motorways. Maybe the half of ours are three-lane, and these roughly are okay. The big trucks swing out very suddenly into the middle doing around one-twenty, but at least you still have an overtaking lane. But if there are only two, and often six-seven trucks nose to tail, you haven't much margin. The fast-brothers are up behind you every moment, the big Mercedes, not to speak of some tin-can samba-wagon with his foot to the floor. There was nothing wrong with John's driving. He was nipping in and out, a good rhythm, around one-thirty they said, which is just right. My brother came up and crowded him, pinching him in towards the emergency lane, to force him to stop. Lights flashing, klaxon going. Dangerous, reckless, use any word you like.

Beyond the emergency-lane is the ditch, right? Has to be, for drainage. I need not spell it out. They were all three killed. Even for us, a bad one. I have seen the photos. Later they called me, to identify the bodies. The patrol blocked the slow lane, for some three hours, to measure. Reckless Jo was, and it's unforgiveable anyhow. Except by me. Technically he was an excellent driver, extremely quick reaction times. Yes, the pills. Yes, plainly, he was in a highly over-excited state. I still didn't believe that left to himself this would have happened. The patrolmen say this too. She wrenched at his arm, or maybe the wheel, in an effort to hold clear, and he over-corrected? The patrol – and the Kripo – have raised a suicide hypothesis. I've said, I'm not accepting any of that. It isn't our business to raise theories or to hold opinions. Nor homicide neither. Judge Not, said Jesus maybe, or Plato. Say I.

My conscience is not clear. I'll come back to this. I have committed crimes, for which a court would condemn me to prison, lacking any better means of punishing me. If they knew. That is one reason for writing this letter. I'm not a shy violet. I'm a man, and I want to be able to stand up.

There are books, one doesn't have to read them, and there are movies, and television serials, one doesn't have to look at, to know. These are full up with every sort of violence the imagination can dream up. They do well, have a lot of success. The more ingeniously base, then the more success. We are a dirty crowd. An accident on the Autobahn, a car upside down in the ditch, all the people hang out of the window, gawking. So fascinated, they've been known to cause a further accident. The same with a fire, the more if inside a burning house there are people, trapped. The professionals learn to block their emotions, or they couldn't do their job. The police and the firemen, who see things we cannot cope with. The Medical Examiner, and the woman in the State Pathology office, who get the small children, raped, burned, tortured. The nurses, who look after lunatics. And the plain good, kindly, who wash and feed and talk to the old men, who sit there senile, farting all the time.

John said, somewhere, whatever the imagination can picture, the human being will go beyond. The unimaginable.

I am the only one left, three generations of us. Not true, there's my aunt, Cathy, more like a sister. In case it came into your mind, no, we don't sleep together. For fear of incest? No, it just doesn't occur to either of us. Now Alan is of course my uncle and it's as though he belonged to a different family.

I still have to go back, to the beginning of John's notebook, to say what I did. Not Why. I don't know why.

I had better make it quite clear that Sibylle had nothing to do with our persecution of John. I can't tell just what she knew about all this. She was good at getting to know things, and at keeping quiet about what she knew. She had an uncanny trick of telling what was in one's mind. She didn't know about this. We saw to that. She wouldn't have harmed a hair on his head. She wouldn't have admitted any damage to things belonging to him. I'd say allowed. We were grown-up, but she had a lot of authority. We were a bit frightened of her, I think more than if she'd been our real mother. Very loving, and could be icy, disapproving. We got into the habit of keeping things secret. I have a bit of explaining to do.

We were still children, when our father killed himself. Gunther rescued us. As you know by now this was his nature. You'd almost say habit. Around this time, it's vague in my mind because we didn't know or understand, Sibylle came back to live with us. Barbara was already ill. Sibylle took on the responsibility of being mother to us so naturally that we hardly noticed. We were happy, where before we hadn't been happy. Finding things out, and getting them wrong, in fragments, this was one of our first ideas about 'John'. We hated him because we thought he'd been cruel to Sibylle.

After Gunther's brother Rudi died, who had the farm, we were rich. Gunther understood the law, knew all the ways of the Administration, succession rights or tax devices, and he knew how not to be hassled. He fixed things so that Sibylle, and ourselves, should never be in want. As students we were pretty comfortable, and if we took time off it was no problem. And we had plenty of ready money.

I need to be careful here. It's too easy to blame everything on Joachim, who is dead. It's true that he was the older and the brighter, and the more decisive, and that I tagged along and I admired, but I mustn't minimise what I did, nor try to excuse it.

We had built up a lot of idiot fixed ideas by then, about John. We blamed him just for existing. We thought he'd abandoned his child by Barbara, our father, and was somehow answerable for all the calamities when we were small. He was 'the Englishman', 'the enemy'. We thought he hated us. And that he'd brought nothing but evil to our much-loved Sibylle. I don't know what we didn't get in our heads. The more, because she never complained, never said anything spiteful. We brooded.

Bit by bit we thought of a lot of dirty tricks. Threats, pressured to cause anguish. Clever words. Legal terms exist. Bringing people into fear, or disrepute, endangering by suggestion. We thought ourselves justified, and we thought ourselves very funny.

There is a lot of crime nowadays of this sort. Not covered by statute, provision in the penal code. Even if proved a court doesn't much sanction many of these things. Misdemeanour. Phoning late at night and breathing down the line. Spreading scandal by insinuation, leaving dead cats on the doorstep. Mean-minded petty stuff. We thought we could do better than that. This word is used a lot – 'destabilise'.

We knew where John lived. We wormed, seeming innocent, a lot of stuff out of Sibylle about the house, how it was fixed, where the Peartrees lived. We went up there for a weekend, scouting about thinking ourselves very tough and crafty.

It was my idea shooting at him to 'just miss'. Ignoble and we thought ourselves immensely funny. See him skip. Creeping down the road with the big pistol – hilarious. Once the idea of scaring him witless took hold we got excited. Knock him loose, make him run for it. We had two cars. Shepherd him along.

Schoolboy spy-novel stuff. It was so easy. I can't put words to my shame. Wandering there through France, the three of us. We had no idea of causing him real harm at that stage. To think now, that this would bring about his death, I am still dodging this.

Joachim got increasingly skilful at guessing his mind. It was Jo who got ahead of him over that ferry port in Brittany which looked like a bolt hole and had that way out to England.

There's very little I can find to exonerate that. Yes, that was Jo. We were both strung up, short of sleep, we had got quite exhausted over the tracking act. I see now that Jo was taking more and more of those pills he had, to stay ahead. I don't know enough about tolerances acquired to speak with certainty about an overdose. I think that Jo got the horrible idea that frightening him wasn't enough, we wouldn't be able to pursue him in England and we'd gone to all this trouble for no real result. I don't know. I feel sure that Jo did not mean to kill him, but that a real bullet, a real wound, would be success, and satisfaction.

I was down at the harbour, to see whether John would get on the ferry. Joachim really must have been insane at that moment. And to get the wrong man – that was infinitely worse than any fiasco we could either of us imagine.

Our one idea was to get out of that hole before the police caught up with us. A blind panic. Jo kept saying the fellow wasn't badly hurt. I think in fact he did recover all right, but we weren't to know that. We quarrelled, furiously. I'd been taking some of those pills myself. I feel ill just thinking about this time. I have to try to be honest with myself. I think I was off my own trolley but there is no excuse, none whatsoever. No extenuating circumstances, nothing to cover the evil we had done. And what had we achieved? Grievous injury, to a harmless innocent bystander.

What I find now especially horrible is that this wasn't at all the way of it at that moment. Not shame but humiliation, that we'd made monkeys of ourselves. I daresay you know about our gangs. The skinheads in big boots. The bare arms with tattoos. The yobs who parade with flags, bawling nazi slogans. Well of course you do, because they get us a lot of bad publicity – and that is just what they like. People say, look at these awful bloody Germans, they don't alter. The idiots love that, they want to be ba-ad and it gives them a big lift to be thought bad and mad and dangerous. They're full of beer and that helps them feel important. When they do something bad, like fire-raising, and women and children are killed, then they get astonished and say they never meant it. You've noticed – when cemeteries get profaned, tombstones broken? Not always Jewish, either. The police have learned to look for small children. Maybe only ten years old. They'll say they were only playing. And it's true.

It is shattering to see and to know that we were exactly on this level. And we are students. We are supposed to be the pick of the bunch. We are not mentally retarded. We've had the best education the country can give us. We have good housing, good homes, lots of everything we could want. No mother could have been more loving than was Sibylle.

I split up with Joachim. I never even knew he had a pistol. You can buy them easily enough on the black market but what would the idiot want with a pistol?

Like some scrawny little boy you see in Africa, with a steel helmet much too big for him. He's got an assault rifle, it's all he has to be proud of.

So Jo was not with me when I burned the house. I alone am answerable.

I was mad. Mad too in the American sense, mad at everything. Mad too still at John, totally childish, we had prepared this most elaborate intimidation thing and it had fizzled into this fiasco, I stampeded off, exactly like the hooligan, saying let's give the Turks a jump then, let's make a bang. There were we running away with the police after us and John gets off with a bit of a fright. No satisfaction in that and less still thinking of the poor fellow in hospital. Pills. One half of my mind was saying, childish foolish frolic ended badly. And the other half still saying, but we wanted to punish John. There's the yob mentality for you, punish the Turks for taking away the job we haven't got, that's their idea of logic.

I thought myself clever. No petrol of course or anything that would look criminal. I wanted it to be Mysterious. All that dry wood, bit of old hay, toss in a fag-end like any careless passer-by. There was a bit of a wind, make a merry blaze. Just to set the woodpile alight, I *think* that was all I wanted. Or am I lying again? That there was too much wind, and inevitably the house would catch – obvious, but I don't *think* this was in my mind. I was in too much of a hurry because I was frightened, damned scared of Peartree and his dogs. Did I want, subliminally, to burn the house? I quite honestly don't know.

I went straight home. I had no more speed pills left, either. You think you can catch up on sleep, after, but you don't, really, and this helps keep you hooked, it's a classic example of 'Flucht nach voren', I don't think you can say that in English, can you?

I was sour with Jo. He didn't get back for several days. John seemed to think we followed him to Amsterdam but in that state of mind one sees things behind every window. The trick in Budapest was all Jo's. How he got on to that I do not know, because we didn't talk to each other for a while. I have to admit it was brilliant, much more what we had originally thought up, but the opportunity has to present itself. I still think it harmless and much more typical of what my brother was really like. Afterwards, when we were friends again, it became a giggle. 'I was really foxy,' was all he would say. What I now know I got from Kollo. Yes, I went to see him. Got on well with him. He's a now-you-see-him, now-you-don't. A mix, which I don't pretend to understand, and certainly I'm no judge. He's genuine in this much anyhow, that he truly does refuse child-abuse. At least I think he does. John would have known and it's hard to see how they would be friendly if . . . I'm not a theologian.

This anyhow he thought extremely comic. Jo, you have to recall, was bigger than me, much cleverer, and a lot better-looking too. He talked himself into a job in the 'roxy'. Like Kollo says, studs are expendable. He was in on one of the romps. I don't know if he got to roger Daffodil, that would be a bit too good and I can see one has to discount most of what they tell you, fast talkers one and all and Kollo not the most backward. This much seems true, that the status as performer got him a room in that hotel and some (enough) of a clue to Daffodil's movements. All the staff knew what went on. They always do, and are well paid to look the other way. I think it was just a matter of an extra bribe, and telling the floor waiter this was an elaborate joke, to 'scare the knickers off ol' Daff'.

Kollo says he got on to this afterwards. He didn't take it seriously. The huff and puff was to save face and soothe vanity.

I don't want to sound a prude or a hypocrite. A handful of dollars – it's all cash in that business, just like cattle-dealing, and it's easy-come, easy-go. I imagine since I haven't tried that fucking those girls is less fun than one might guess. What effect has a speed pill there? I wouldn't know. My own experience was such a kick in the balls I'll not be anxious for another. When I said who I was, Kollo was hospitable with a lot of drinks, and, 'You don't let them have any at work'. I didn't get offered any jobs.

Better get me straight. My girl and I are a very ordinary couple indeed. We do like to drink, and to go to bed together. I have looked up most of the references in the notebook. Like Mr Pepys. I'd say, that if I were to behave that way, then she would act pretty much the way Mrs Pepys did. Saying that in this Restoration time morals were easy-going, this doesn't impress me much. Those women sound extremely modern to me.

After all, nothing much changes, the world stutters on as best it can, happenings seem dramatic, and they're quickly forgotten. I went to see Brigitta, who told me that whatever sound and fury she and her friends were able to muster for the last days before the tenth anniversary means prescription, when all hypothetical criminal charges become automatically null and void, they never managed to pin down responsibilities for Palme's assassination. So that story is still there, waiting for John to make something of it in fiction. It was very much up his street.

She told me another story, that when it happened she had been sleeping with John, more or less openly, and that she'd overheard at a party his publisher talking to one of those chalky old men who have much influence with the Nobel committee, and saw to it that Greene would never get it. The old boy glanced at her and said (intending to be heard), 'Isn't that Charles' whore?' The publisher made a good answer. 'She would I think choose so to describe herself.' Brigitta said she felt a moment of pride.

I've been to see a lawyer. I don't know any, but found a name in the book I recognised as the son of a man Gunther was friendly with. He listened quietly, laughing to see me in a fluster. These stories (he said) which appear as complicated, weird, are lawyers' daily bread. There are hundreds such. Until the last of those who lived through the war are gone. And the occupation. And their children. And those who live in the East. And those who were flung out by the Czechs. And now – where will Serbia end, and Croatia begin? And where exactly is Bosnia? Do you know? Lawyers aren't short of business. And we, I mean the ones my age, the students, who thought we could turn the page and start afresh with no hangovers, can't. Because we too are part of European history.

John's affairs belong to a French court. Alan will look after them. Sibylle's, since they never divorced, are in the same boat. On the 'property' here, the heritage of Gunther, he says he'll get a court order, and that I need have no worries. As long as the lawyers are paid . . . We have nigh as many as in the States.

I went to my professor, who was unfussed and said,

'Take a year off.' He gave me too an introduction to
the Professor of Latin. I've tried to verify references,
and knowing no Latin (I must mend that) I couldn't
make much of John's bits-of-quote. Nice old man.
Laughed a lot, said that it threw some interesting light
upon John's character. And he gave me another line,
which I'm keeping for the end of this. It seemed a
good 'epilogue'.

I needn't have bothered. I went to see Cathy. She
knows Latin. This was good, because she told me to
come back, again and often. She likes being 'my
Spanish aunt'. Yes, I like being her German 'brother'.

Alan and Steph in France have also become friends.
I'm in the family. That's as it should be.

The professor rambled somewhat, forgot I think that
I wasn't one of his own students, started telling me 'the
sort of thing English schoolchildren would have had in
those days.' You must correct this if I got it wrong
because I'm citing him from memory, but 'big chunks
of Aeneid and the more imperial odes of Horace,'
after 'a good grounding in Caesar and maybe a little
Ovid.' Very imperial – 'fitting them to rule the Master
Race' – is that a bit naughty? They 'wouldn't have had
the sexy bits, naked slave girls putting logs on Horace's
fire.' I think it was this that made him veer off into
telling me about a lyric 'ascribed to Virgil and so
unlike him that it probably *is* Virgil' about a Syrian
dancing girl.

I've gone into this detail because he forgot I knew
no Latin and when I reminded him put it in colloquial
German, so putting that now into English I'm making
mistakes? Perhaps that doesn't matter? John with his
English upbringing and his German wife and Spanish
daughter might have said, Never mind all these

peasant dialects we talk but get the European Essence right. So I wrote the Latin down and asked the old man to see I'd had it right.

> *Pone merum et talos, pereat qui crastina curat.*
> *Mors aurem vellens, 'vivite' ait, 'venio'.*

Which is, approximately Put down (lay down?) the wine-cup and the dice, and go hang thinking about tomorrow. Death is twitching (would it be?) me by the ear. 'Live', he says, 'I'm arriving'.

I don't know whether John knew this, but I thought it just his style.

Yours sincerely,
Christian

(Wade)

Yes, I do like it, which is why I've left this in. Incidentally, I think that 'Set down' would be the accepted English for 'Pone'. It was a little bit before my time but certainly this 'old boy' wasn't far out and the bluffer kinds of public school, which I should think really were all exactly like this, right up to 1939. Little had changed since the schoolmasters described by Orwell or Cyril Connolly. One must try and remember that John's early formative years were in this mould, that 'the awful relations' he mentions, Robert's family, were indeed the empire-building master-race against which he would revolt so violently. Even after the war. I suppose that a historian would now point to Eden's notorious Suez adventure as the traumatic breaking-off. To this day, one is tempted to say, there would be plenty to yap at the heels of the 'German woman', the mother he could scarcely remember. With a name like Magda – seriously, could one, today, imagine an English child being christened 'Magdalena'? to be persecuted out of her mind by schoolfellows. One quite often wonders whether the xenophobia, the parochial jingoism, the talk about 'Squareheads', ever in historic times reached a higher flood level than it does at this moment.

I was not at the end of my surprises. A letter came to me, neatly typed but rather in the style of the signature, which was female, boldly legible and yes, a bit school-mistressy. She had even used a red felt-tip pen to sign, so that one suspected she'd been correcting the children's exercises and had picked it up without noticing.

Dear Mr Wade,
I think that by this time you have received and will
have had time to read the manuscript notebook left

behind by my father, John Charles. I agreed that this should be sent to you, perhaps even published. This is still a one-sided picture, and you should know a little more, before reaching a decision.

Christian came to see me, perturbed by what he feels as guilt, and with some questions. One was to ask whether my mother 'fled' from the house and from an overwhelming personality. No.

After much battle and doubt, persuaded that she had a life of her own to live, and that this could never be realised, she left after long thought. A proud woman, and the picture of a stubborn, dull, slow-witted one does not do her justice. She was also profoundly religious, with small time for churches, clerics, or accepted dogmas. There are many such, and not just in Spain.

He asked whether she had never come to see me. Of course. She would not cut herself from her children. She also saw my brothers. Jaimie perhaps had no great sympathy with my father's viewpoint. Alan rather more so. I told Christian that women have their secretive little ways.

Perhaps it should be emphasized that she refused to take any money from my father. Gunther, whom I am sorry not to have known, took pains well before his death to ensure that she should not be in need. I saw her often, and once we spent a happy fortnight's holiday together.

About the crisis provoked by learning of the 'incest' (being half-sister to her husband): I did not know of this. Her sense of family was strong. Her own children had grown up, stable human beings. She resolved that the second half of her life should be given to these boys, unhappy through no fault of theirs nor hers.

I never met Barbara. I could guess at guilt and anxiety in my father. I knew nothing of my half-brother.

Impersonally, I find Gunther at fault in telling Sibylle of the long-buried accident of her parentage. I conclude with a great sympathy for this man, who, his life long, upheld the good and the right. Perhaps he felt close to his death, and the need to unburden was too much for him. He would have had confidence in her common sense. I feel sure that she was unbalanced only by the unhappy series of events, the boys' rather terrifying plot to pursue and persecute John. I don't think that Christian ever clearly understood what they had set afoot. He certainly never 'envisaged' the possible consequences. It is plain that the elder brother was a psychiatrist's field day. In the world no less than in Germany are many such people, who cannot face the dark side of their selves, and who create the havoc we read of in virtually any copy of any newspaper.

I have to hypothesise that my beloved mother could not handle the double strain of Joachim's violence. I am no expert on prolonged intake of amphetamines but have seen other examples, and very nasty they can be. I should suppose you must have similar experiences. And of this fear of incest, traumatic to a woman of that background and upbringing (still much that was Calvinist about that). Finding John actually under her roof in so dramatic and unplanned fashion (pretty 'steep', we'll agree) she found it too much for her. She would, I am persuaded, have attempted her double aim. To ask that he take on a share of responsibility for the boys, in order to heal the breach caused by their father's failings. And to accept, at last, the independence of spirit which was her birthright.

My father's euphoric suggestion towards sexual relations (she was a still-beautiful and desirable woman, her age meant little) was I think a bit-too-much, for her.

Are you thinking, Mr Wade, 'what a frightful female'? I am untroubled. You will find, in Europe, hundreds of thousands of woman as chilly-seeming. In romantic terms such as many men credit us with, a refusal to compromise is often thought a Spanish trait. Neither in Germany nor in England could I accept that this so-called 'ruthlessness' would be in the least strange.

In my reading, not long ago, was Maurois' book on Proust. Maurois has no sort of reputation nowadays, but a passage caught my attention which I believe throws light upon Sibylle as well as on John.

'Human beings, as a rule, accept glory and love and the triumphs of the world at their face value. Proust, declining to do so, is led on to seek an absolute that lies outside this world and outside Time itself. It is the absolute that religious mystics find in God. Proust, for his part, looks for it in art, thereby practising a form of mysticism that is closer to the other than might be supposed, because all art in its origins was religious, and because religion has often found in art the means of communicating to the human consciousness truths which the intelligence can discover only with difficulty.' (Maurois: *A la recherche de Marcel Proust*, translated by Gerard Hopkins. Jonathan Cape, 1950)

Yours truly
Catherine Charles

(Wade)
It is evident that this script, once edited and readied for printing, will show a good deal of variation from the disjointed notes of the original. The decision whether or not to publish will also depend on a formal clearance from this lady and her brothers, John's heirs. Speaking for myself I believe that both 'Cathy' and 'Christian' have indeed found worthwhile tributes to my old friend.

London, 1998